Mr. Ferdinand Fisk, Cat Detective

Story and Pictures
by Tony Linsell

McGraw-Hill Book Company
New York   St. Louis   San Francisco

Library of Congress Cataloging
in Publication Data

Linsell, Tony.
Mr. Ferdinand Fisk, cat detective.

SUMMARY: The famous cat detective is called in on a
missing animals case.
[1. Animals—Fiction.   2. Mystery and detective
stories]   I. Title.
PZ7.L66317Mi   1979   [E]   79-12422
ISBN 0-07-037950-5

First published and distributed in the United States of
America 1979 by McGraw-Hill Book Company

First published in Great Britain 1979 by Evans Brothers
Limited, Montague House, Russell Square, London
WC1B 5BX, England

Published by arrangement with Evans Brothers Limited

Printed in Great Britain

123456789   7832109

One evening Arnold Vole sat peacefully smoking his pipe, when three large, gray creatures appeared. Suddenly one of them popped a net over Arnold's head and carried him quickly away.

Soon Arnold's friends heard that he was missing. Other animals had disappeared too.
Where had they gone?

A meeting was called to discuss the mystery. Jerry Jackdaw suggested that they ask the famous cat detective, Mr. Ferdinand Fisk, for help.
Harry, the big-eyed rabbit, was sent scurrying off to fetch him.

Harry was a little afraid of meeting the great cat detective, but Mr. Ferdinand Fisk listened carefully to his story, scratching his head as he did so.

Ferdinand
Fisk
(Detective)
Special Rates
after 6 p.m.

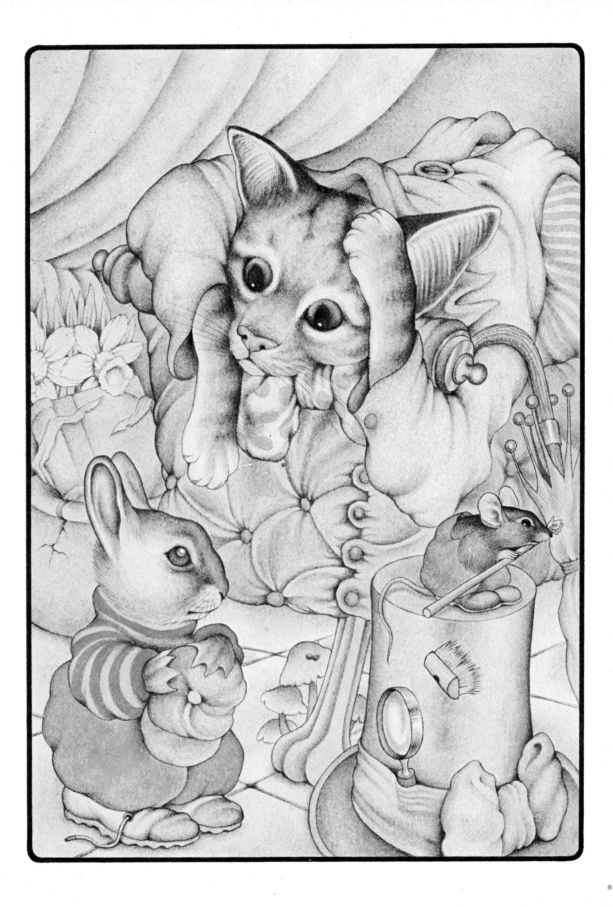

Suddenly he jumped up and rushed the startled rabbit outside to his bicycle. Attached to the bicycle was a sidecar. Mr. Fisk picked Harry up, dumped him into the sidecar, and pedaled furiously down to the riverbank. They went so fast that Harry nearly fell out!

At the riverbank, the animals made a great fuss over Ferdinand Fisk. The great detective was very pleased and asked them to show him where Arnold Vole had been sitting when he disappeared.

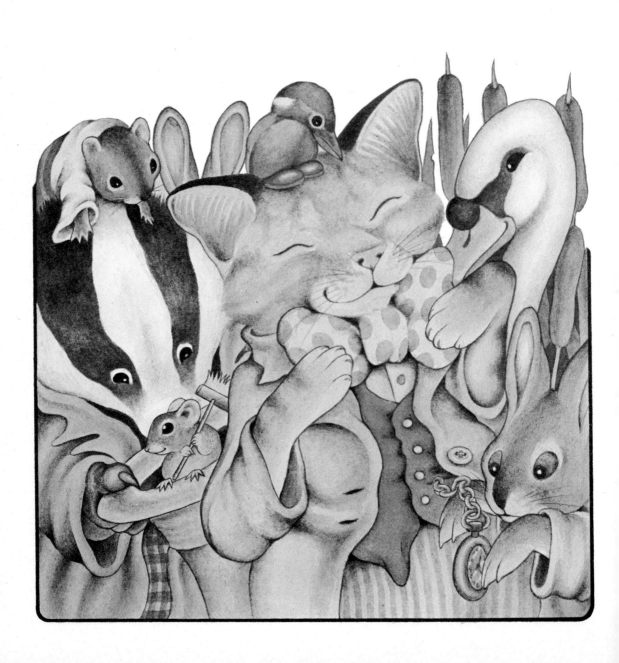

Mr. Fisk searched carefully in and around the grass and flowers that grew by the river. He looked closely at the mud on the riverbank. He even looked at Maggie Mouse very suspiciously through his large magnifying glass.

Soon he gave a triumphant shout and pointed with an excited paw at a neat, star-shaped footprint in the mud.

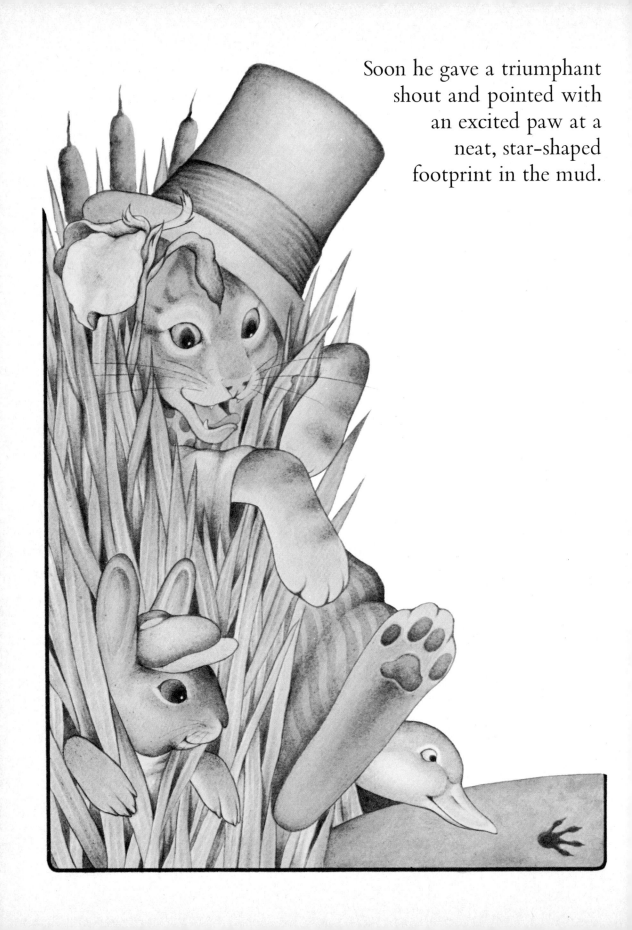

Mr. Fisk pulled a map out of his pocket. With an elegant claw he followed the river until he came to a dark shape, marked "Old Cottage: Vacant."

"Aha!" he cried. Then he signaled for Harry to follow him.

The excited rabbit and the great Mr. Fisk set off along the riverbank. Mrs. Vole heard them tramping along overhead as she sipped a hot mug of tea.

Soon they came to the vacant cottage marked on Mr. Fisk's map. Slates were missing from the roof and the glass in the window frames was broken.

But a thin wisp of smoke rose from a cracked chimney pot, and by the old front gate, noisily chewing a bacon sandwich, stood a fat, greasy rat.

At the back of the house, Harry explored some huge wooden boxes. Suddenly he stepped on an old roof slate. It broke with a snap.

The fat rat
pricked up his ears.
He looked at Harry
and growled,
"Buzz off, or else…"

Harry rushed back to
Mr. Fisk. He told him
what he had seen
written on top of the
large wooden boxes.
There were the
terrifying words:
BROWN'S
PET FOOD
FACTORY!

"Aha! As I thought," said Mr. Fisk, his whiskers twitching. "Tonight, Harry, with the help of the full moon, we'll solve the case."

So that evening, by the light of the moon, Mr. Ferdinand Fisk and Harry returned to the cottage. They crept forward quietly for a closer look.

From inside the cottage came the noise of singing and shouting. Five rowdy rats were having a party. "The animal-stealers," whispered Mr. Fisk.

The fat rat they had seen before was still by the front door. But now he was snoring loudly. Ferdinand Fisk crept softly up to him.

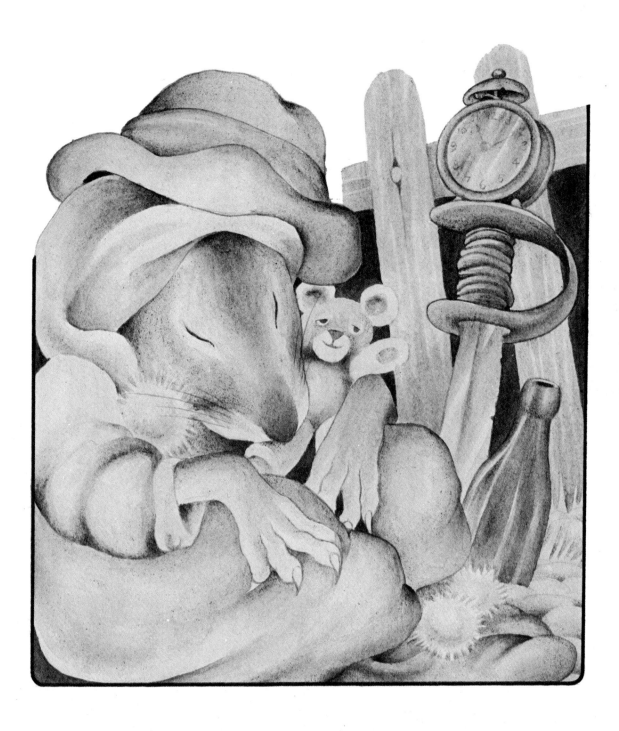

He threw his top hat over the rat's head. Then he neatly turned the hat, rat and all, upside down. All the rat could do was kick his legs in the air. Hatless, Mr. Fisk sped off to where the big boxes were stacked at the back of the cottage.

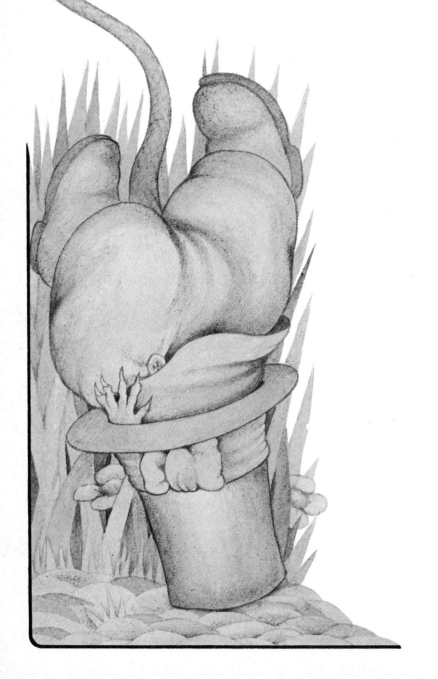

"Harry, use your teeth," Mr. Fisk ordered.
Harry bit through the ropes tied around the boxes, and out popped a shrew, two moles, a young rabbit, a woodmouse, and, lastly, Arnold Vole.
The missing animals had been found.

"Quickly! Off you go with Harry," whispered the detective. So Harry packed all the animals on Mr. Fisk's bicycle and cycled away.

Meanwhile Mr. Ferdinand Fisk crept back to the front door of the cottage and pinned a note on it. It read:

Dear Sir,

   Some cat friends of mine (about six in number) will be popping in tomorrow in the hope that you will be able to offer them hospitality while they do a little hunting in the area!

   I hope you will be able to help them.

                    Yours faithfully

                    F. F. (Cat)

Then he went to rescue his beautiful hat.
When the rat saw a large cat holding
him by the tail, he struggled to free
himself and sped away into the night.
He was never seen again!

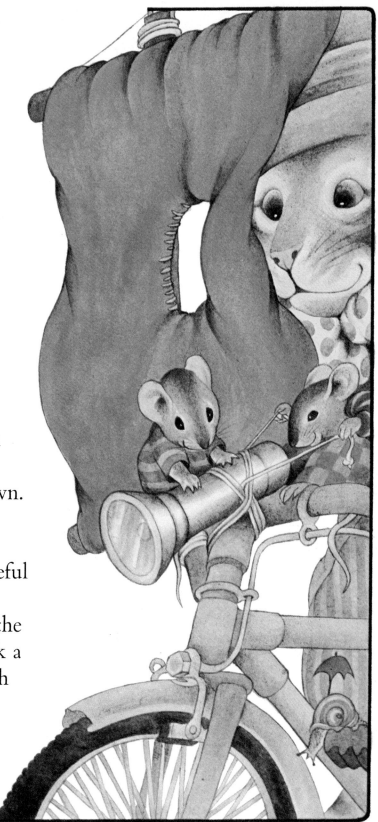

By the time Mr. Fisk
returned to the
riverbank, it was dawn.
He and Harry were
welcomed as heroes.
Harry showed his useful
teeth to anyone who
was interested. And the
animals gave Mr. Fisk a
large flashlight, which
they tied to the
handlebars of his
wonderful bicycle.

The animals cheered and waved as Mr. Fisk pedaled away.

But on his way home he looked in at the cottage to make sure that his plan had really worked.

It had. The cottage was now deserted. A half-eaten meal and an overturned chair told of a hurried departure.

Because if there is one thing in the whole, wide world that rats do not like, it is a sleek, fine-whiskered cat detective!

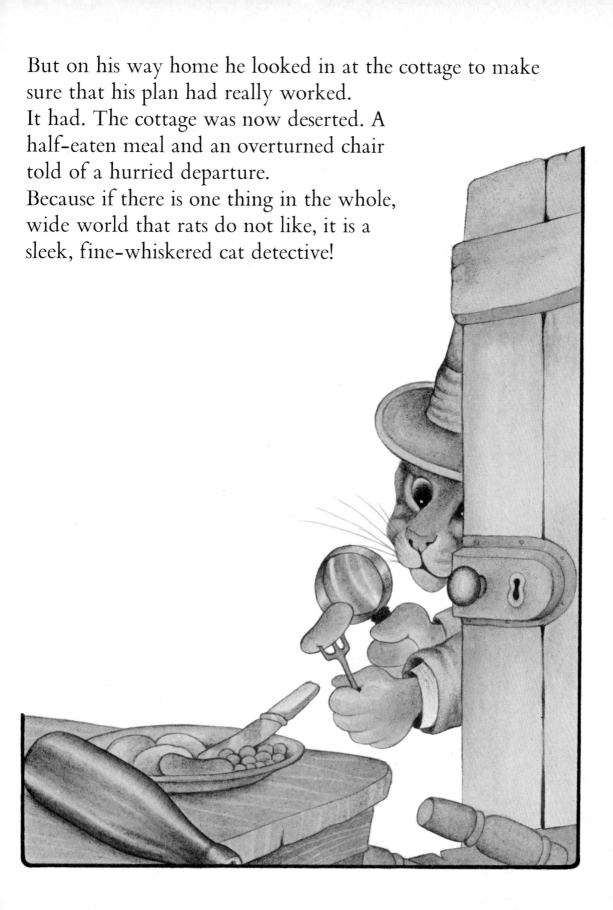

Mr. Fisk was now content
that he had solved the case
and so he waved his hat gaily
at everyone as he cycled
slowly home.

AGES 3-5

SUPER SIMPLE BIBLE LESSONS

60
Ready-to-Use
Bible Activities

Abingdon Press

Nashville

Abingdon's
SUPER SIMPLE BIBLE LESSONS
60 Ready–to–Use Bible Activities
Ages 3–5

0-687-49770-1

ART BY ROBERT S. JONES.

05 06 07 08 09 10 11 12 13 14—10 9 8 7 6 5 4 3 2 1
MANUFACTURED IN THE UNITED STATES OF AMERICA

TABLE OF CONTENTS

How to use this resource

Sometimes all you need is a Bible story that is ready to tell and a simple craft or game that requires almost nothing at all to do it. If you've ever heard yourself say this, then this resource is for you!

Super Simple Bible Lessons is a quick trip through the Bible, from Genesis to the letters of Paul. Each lesson contains these elements:

1. A Bible story
2. A Bible verse to learn
3. A Bible story-related activity (craft or game)

At the back of the book is a Scripture index if you would like to coordinate the stories here with other stories you may be using with the children. Also available from Abingdon Press is a corresponding resource for children ages six to eight.

The activities included in this resource require minimal supplies, most of which are available to you in the typical church school classroom or may be easily obtained from the church office.

Basic Supplies

photocopier	white glue	crayons and markers
construction paper	stapler, staples	masking tape
string or yarn	paper lunch bags	clear tape
scissors	pencils	wooden craft sticks
cardboard	cotton swabs	tissue paper
baby oil	cotton balls	sandpaper
envelopes	tempera paint	recycled newspaper
fabric scraps	small containers	aluminum foil
ribbon	paintbrushes	coins
lace	smooth rocks	wooden blocks
curling ribbon	glitter	metallic crayons
gold foil paper	sponge	white or gold doilies
wrapped candies	gel markers	watercolor markers
water	shallow trays	multicultural crayons
tissues	plain white paper	or markers
coverups		

IN THE BEGINNING

by Sharilyn Adair

The Bible

Genesis 1:1–13

And God saw that
it was good.

(Genesis 1:25)

Supplies

white glue
green
   construction
   paper
crayons
markers
cotton swabs
small containers

Bible Story

Ssh! Lie down and close your eyes. Be very still. Let's pretend that we are lying like a big pool of water at the very beginning of the world. Everything is dark and quiet. We can't see anything or hear anything. Let's listen to how quiet it is. *(Pause.)*

At first we don't feel anything. But then God breathes fresh air over us. We don't peek because the world is still dark. And we can't see anything. *(Pause.)*

Now God has decided to make two different times— nighttime for sleeping and daytime for seeing things and running and playing. You may sit up and when I say "Night is day," open your eyes. When I say "Now it is night," close your eyes.

God wants the world to have a big blue sky over it. Stand up and reach high over your head. Pretend that your hands are the sky. God sees that the sky is good.

God has decided to make land in the water. You might be a big tall mountain or a long flat beach full of sand. God likes the land and water.

God wants the land to be beautiful. God makes plants and trees grow on the land. *(Pretend to be plants.)* God likes the plants and trees. God has made a beautiful world. Let's say "hooray" for God's world.

Creative Fun

Pour a small amount of white glue into small containers. You will need one container for each pair of children. Make a copy of the tree on the following page for each child. Have the children color the tree trunk and the branches. Then tear construction paper in different shades of green into small thumb-size shapes. Have the children paint the top of the tree with white glue using a cotton swab, then place the construction paper pieces on the tree to become leaves.

7

FILLING THE EARTH

by Sharilyn Adair

The Bible

Genesis 1:20-25

And God saw that
it was good.
(Genesis 1:25)

Supplies

scissors
envelopes

Bible Story

When God shaped the earth and planted the trees
 the skies still looked empty and so did the seas.
God knew what to do; so God filled up the sky
 with all kinds of creatures that knew how to fly.
There were eagles and thrushes and whippoorwills, too.
There were blackbirds and red birds and birds that were
 blue.
There were crows and canaries and big birds called fowls.
And for flying at night God created the owls (Whooo.)

The sky was now filled and so was the sea,
 So God looked around to think what else could be.
So God made some cows and some pigs and some goats.
God made some lizards and 'gators and stoats.
God made the tigers and lions and bears.
God made the zebras and monkeys and hares.
God made mosquitoes and bees that would buzz.
God made caterpillars all covered with fuzz.
All of the creatures that now live in this land,
 Were all a part of God's wonderful plan.

Creative Fun

Make two copies of the pictures of the animals on the
following page. Cut them apart and put them in an
envelope. Let the children try to match the different
creatures.

8

9

IN GOD'S IMAGE

by Sharilyn Adair

The Bible

Genesis 1:26-27, 31

God made us, and we belong to God.
(Psalm 100:3, Good News Translation, adapted)

Supplies

glue
construction
   paper
yarn
trim
fabric
scissors

Bible Story

In the beginning of everything, God made a beautiful world. God worked and worked to make it just right.

God made the sky and filled it with shiny things, like the sun, moon, and stars. And all those things were good.

But still God was not through. God made water into oceans and caused land to be separated from the water. And those things were good.

But still God was not through. God covered the land with green plants and trees and grasses. And all those things were good.

But still God was not through. God filled the water with fishes and sea animals, and God filled the sky with birds. And all those things were good.

But still God was not through. God filled the land with all kinds of animals and creepy, crawly things. And all those things were good.

But still God was not through. "I have created a beautiful world," God said, "but something is missing. I need some-body to take care of my world, somebody who can plant seeds for more plants to grow and who can watch over my trees. I need somebody who can take care of the birds and the fish and the animals. I need somebody just like me."

So God made people. God made men and women to take care of the plants and animals and land. And then God was through making the world. And God saw everything that was made, especially the people who were made to be like God. And, indeed, everything God had made was very, very good.

Creative Fun

Make a copy of the figure on the following page. Provide a variety of decorating supplies, such as construction paper, yarn, trim, and fabric. Have the children create a figure that will represent themselves. Remind them that they were created in God's image.

10

THE VERY BIG BOAT

by Daphna Flegal

The Bible

Genesis 6:9–7:17;
Genesis 7:24–8:22; 9:13

Trust in the LORD.
(Psalm 37:3)

Supplies

crayons
markers
masking tape

Bible Story

"Noah," said God, "I want you to build a very big boat." Noah obeyed God.

Zzz. Zzz. Noah cut the wood to build a very big boat. **Bam, Bam, Bam** went the hammer. Noah hammered the wood to build a very big boat.

Finally the very big boat was finished.

"Noah," said God, "I want you to put two of every animal on this very big boat."

Baa. Baa. Noah brought two sheep into the very big boat. **Moo. Moo.** Noah brought two cows into the very big boat. **Roar. Roar.** Noah brought two lions into the very big boat. **Squeak. Squeak.** Noah brought two mice into the very big boat. **Quack, Quack.** Noah brought two ducks into the very big boat. **Neigh. Neigh.** Noah brought two horses into the very big boat. **Coo. Coo.** Noah brought two doves into the very big boat. **Baa. Roar. Quack.** The very big boat was full of animals.

Spitter, spatter. It started to rain. **Spitter spatter.** It rained and rained. **Spitter, spatter.** It rained for forty days and forty nights.

Moo. Squeak. Neigh. Noah, his family, and all the animals were safe and dry inside the very big boat.

Ssh. The rain stopped. **Coo. Coo.** Noah sent out a dove. The dove did not return. Noah knew it was safe to leave the boat. **Baa. Roar. Squeak.** All the animals left the very big boat. **Ooo. Ooo.** Noah and his family looked up into the sky. They saw a beautiful rainbow.

"I promise that I will always care for you," said God. "I have placed my bow across the clouds to help you remember my promise."

Creative Fun

Make a copy of Noah's very big boat for each child. Have them color the boat and add strips of masking tape to the hull of the boat to be the planks of wood.

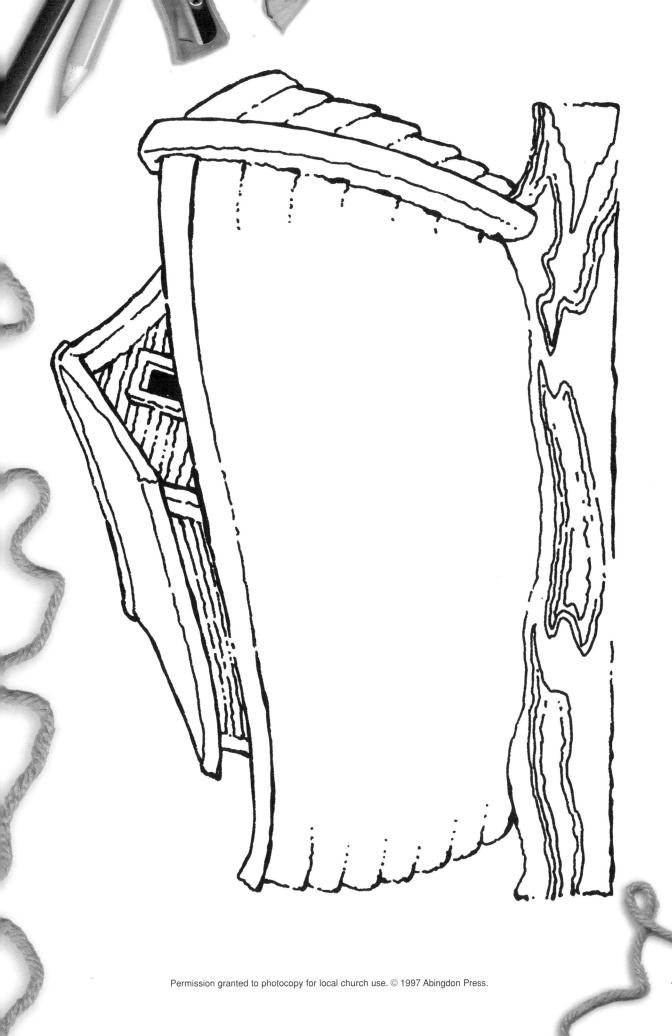

13

ABRAHAM AND SARAH

by Elizabeth Parr

The Bible

Genesis 12:1-8

God said,
"I will bless you."
(Genesis 12:1-2, adapted)

Supplies

markers
crayons
baby oil
small
 containers
cotton swabs
tape

Bible Story

God spoke to Abraham one fine day.
"I want you to move away.
Move to a land that I will show.
Listen now, it's time to go."
God said, "Abraham, I've got good news.
There's a great land that I'll give to you.
I'll bless you and you'll be the dad
Of many children, now aren't you glad?
I'll be with you both night and day.
Trust me now, I'll show the way."

Abraham listened to God that day.
He packed his things and walked away.
Abraham, his wife, Sarah, too,
Did just what God said to do.
They traveled down a dusty road.
They carried their things. What a load!
They weren't afraid because they knew
God said, "I'll always be with you."

Abraham and Sarah saw this beautiful land.
Everything was just like God had planned.
At the big tree they built an altar of stone.
They thanked God that they were not alone.
This land was for them and their family.
God told them so beneath the big tree.

Creative Fun

   Make copies of the picture of Abraham and Sarah,
one for each child. Have the children color the picture with
markers or crayons. Pour a small amount of baby oil in
small containers. Give each child a cotton swab. Once the
picture has been colored, let them dip their swabs into the
oil and rub it over the picture to create a translucent effect.
Hang the pictures in a sunny window.

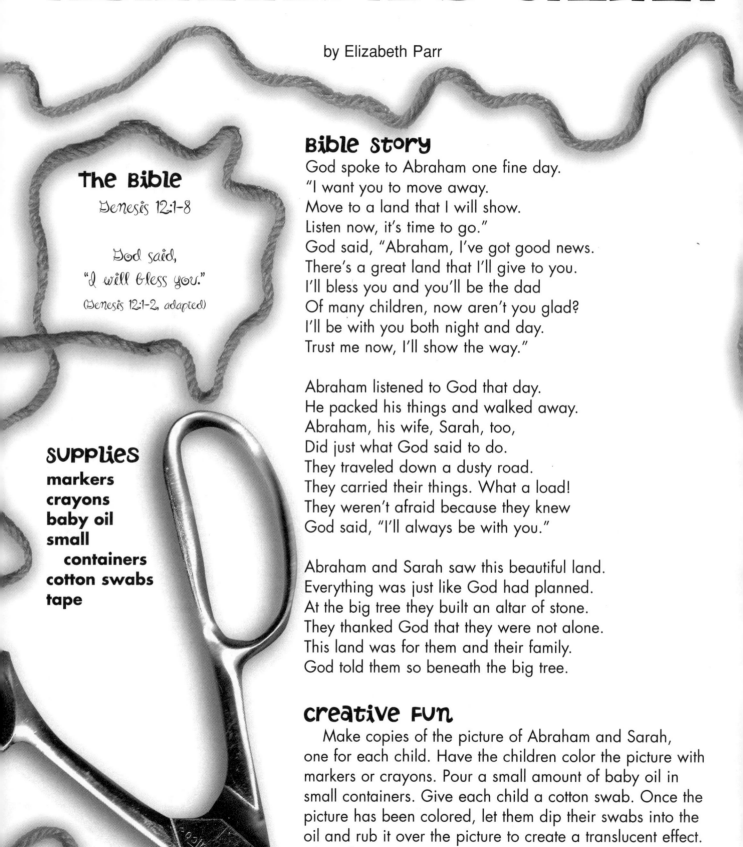

15

SARAH LAUGHS

by Sharilyn Adair

THE BIBLE

Genesis 18:1-15; 21:1-8

God said,
"I will bless you."
(Genesis 12:1-2, adapted)

SUPPLIES

crayons
markers
scissors
wooden craft
sticks
masking tape

CREATIVE FUN

Make a copy of the story figures. Color the figures and cut them out. Mount each figure to a wooden craft stick using masking tape. Hand them out to the children. Identify each of the figures (Abraham, Sarah, the three men). Have the children hold up each figure whenever they hear that character's name mentioned in the story.

BIBLE STORY

Abraham feels happy. He has just had his lunch. His tummy is full of good food and he is resting in the shade of his tent. Abraham laughs a happy laugh.

Oh, look. Three men are coming to visit Abraham. "Welcome, my friends," says Abraham. "Stop awhile and visit with me. Here is some water to wash your feet. Sit under this tree and rest. I will get you some food."

"Thank you," say the three visitors. Abraham rushes into the tent to ask Sarah to bake some bread and cook some food for their guests. Abraham takes food to the three visitors. He stays to talk with them while they eat. The food is good. And Abraham and the three visitors are having a happy time. They all laugh.

Sarah is inside the tent. She listens to the men talking and laughing. "Where is Sarah?" one of the visitors asks.

"Sarah is in the tent," Abraham answers.

"I am coming back this way in nine months," says one of the visitors. "Sarah will have a baby then."

Sarah hears what the visitor says. "How can I have a baby?" Sarah says to herself. "I am old enough to be a grandmother, not a mother. And Abraham is too old too." Sarah laughs to herself.

The visitor says, "Don't laugh. Nothing is too hard for God to do. When I come back to see you, you really will have a baby."

Nine months later, Sarah does have a baby. His name is Isaac. Sarah is so happy, she laughs and laughs and laughs.

ISAAC AND REBEKAH

by Sharilyn Adair

The Bible

Genesis 24:1-67

God said,
"I will bless you."
(Genesis 12:1-2, adapted)

Supplies

tape
crayons
markers
scissors

Bible Story

"Eliezer," said Abraham, "go to my old home and find a wife for my son Isaac."

Eliezer was a servant of Abraham. So he traveled all the way from the land of Canaan to the land of Haran. He stopped his camel outside the city gates. Eliezer made his camel kneel down and Eliezer swung his leg over and slid to the ground.

"How can I find a wife for Isaac?" Eliezer worried. And then he began to pray. He asked God to help him find a wife for Isaac.

Just then Rebekah came out of the city gates. She had a water jar on top of her head. Rebekah went to the well outside the gates and lowered her jar into the well to get some water.

"May I have a drink of water?" Eliezer asked Rebekah. Rebekah tipped her jar for Eliezer to have a drink. Rebekah saw that Eliezer's camels were hot and thirsty.

"I will pour water for your camels," she said.

Slurp. Slurp. The thirsty camels drank. "What a kind person," thought Eliezer. He thanked Rebekah and gave her two bracelets to wear. Then he asked, "What is your name and who are your parents? Do they have room for me and my camels to stay overnight?"

Eliezer went to Rebekah's home. He told her family how Abraham had sent him. He asked if Rebekah could be Isaac's wife. Everyone said yes. And Eliezer gave them gifts from Abraham.

Now Eliezer knew that God had answered his prayer. He had found a wife for Isaac. Eliezer was very happy.

Creative Fun

Make a copy of the bracelets on the following page. Have the children color them and cut them out. Tape the bracelets onto the children's wrists. These bracelets will remind them of how God answered Eliezer's prayer for help.

19

JACOB AND ESAU

by Elizabeth Parr

THE BIBLE

Genesis 25:19-34

Be kind to one another.

(Ephesians 4:32)

SUPPLIES

envelopes
scissors
crayons
markers
glue

CREATIVE FUN

Prepare two envelopes for each child by sealing each envelope and cutting the side out to form a pocket. Make a copy of the hand puppets for each child and invite the children to color them. Remind the children to give Esau red hair. Have the children glue each puppet to an envelope. Have the children slip an envelope on each hand and hold up that puppet as you tell about him in the story.

BIBLE STORY

After Rebekah and Isaac were married, they had two boys who were twins. Their names were Jacob and Esau.

Esau was born first and had lots of red hair. Jacob was the second baby, and he did not have red hair. Even though they were twins, as they got older they liked to do different things.

Esau liked to spend lots of time outdoors. Esau helped his family by hunting and finding food for them to eat. He loved to hear the wind blow through the grasses and watch the animals running through the fields.

Jacob was quiet and liked to be inside the tent where his family lived. Jacob helped his family by cooking food for them to eat. He liked to hear the crackle of the fire that heated the cooking pot. He liked to smell the tasty food he cooked for his family.

One day Jacob was cooking some stew. He stirred the stew as it cooked. He had bowls ready to fill with the delicious stew he was cooking. Jacob's brother, Esau, came in from the fields where he had been hunting. Esau had been hunting all day and was very tired. He was also very, very hungry. He smelled the delicious stew and knew he had to have some of it.

"Please share some of that stew with me," he said, "I am so very hungry." Jacob gave Esau some of the stew.

Jacob and Esau were brothers. Even though they liked different things, God loved them both. Rebekah and Isaac loved them too.

21

JOSEPH'S COAT

by Daphna Flegal

the bible

Genesis 37:12-28

God said, "Remember, I will be with you."
(Genesis 28:15,
Good News Translation, adapted)

supplies

crayons
markers

Bible story

"Look at my new coat!" Joseph called to his brothers. He held out his arms and the long sleeves of his coat and turned around. "It has so many beautiful colors," he said. "It has red and blue and yellow and green colors."

"Where did you get that coat?" asked one of Joseph's brothers.

"Father gave it to me," answered Joseph.

The brothers were not happy about Joseph's coat. They did not like the beautiful colors. They did not like the red, the blue, the yellow, and the green colors. "Father has never given any of us a coat like that," said one brother.

"Father loves Joseph more than he loves us," said another brother. And the brothers decided to do something unkind to Joseph. They tore Joseph's coat with its beautiful colors.

They tore the red, and blue, and yellow, and green colors. Then they pushed Joseph into a big hole.

"Look over there," said one brother. "Do you see that caravan? It's on its way to Egypt."

"Let's sell Joseph to the caravan," said another brother. "They will take him far away to Egypt."

The brothers pulled Joseph out of the hole. Soon Joseph was on his way to Egypt with the caravan. Joseph was afraid, but he remembered his father and the beautiful coat. He remembered the red and blue and yellow and green colors. Joseph also remembered that God was with him.

creative fun

Make a copy of Joseph's coat for each child. Let them decorate the coat with crayons or markers. After everyone is finished, invite the children to "model" their coats.

BABY IN A BASKET

by Elizabeth Parr

the Bible

Exodus 1:1-2:10

God cares for you.

(1 Peter 5:7, adapted)

supplies

crayons
markers
scissors
glue

Bible Story

Rocking, rocking, rocking. *(Sway back and forth.)* Baby Moses was floating in the grass at the edge of the River Nile. His mother had made a little boat out of reeds so that he would be safe. The king was trying to get rid of all the baby boys born to the Israelites.

Rocking, rocking, rocking. *(Sway back and forth.)* Moses' mother put him in the basket. She told his sister to stay nearby and watch him. Baby Moses floated peacefully on the river.

Splash, splash, splash. *(Pretend to splash your face with water.)* The king's daughter had come to the river to take a bath. As she walked by the water, she saw the basket where Moses slept. She told her helpers to pull the basket out of the water.

Waa, waa, waa. *(Rub your eyes like you are crying.)* Baby Moses was crying. The king's daughter felt sorry for him. She knew he was an Israelite baby. Moses' sister came out of her hiding place. She asked the king's daughter if she would like to have someone to take care of the baby.

"Yes, yes," said the princess.

Run, run, run. *(Run in place.)* Moses' sister ran all the way home. She brought her mother back to meet the king's daughter. The king's daughter said, "Take care of this baby for me." Moses' mother was happy to take care of him.

Smile, smile, smile. *(Smile and put fingers at the corners of your mouth.)* Moses' mother took Moses home. She took good care of him. God had taken good care of Moses and his family.

Creative Fun

Make a copy of the picture of Moses and Miriam for each child. Cut out the figure of Miriam. Have the children color the pictures of Miriam and of the baby in the basket. Then have the children glue the picture of Miriam in the reeds where she kept watch over her baby brother.

25

THE BURNING BUSH

by Elizabeth Parr

The Bible

Exodus 3:1-22

God said,
"I will be with you."

(Exodus 3:12, adapted)

Supplies

crayons
markers
scissors
envelopes
construction
paper
glue

Bible Story

Baa. Baa. The sheep were eating some of the plants in the desert. Moses was the shepherd who was taking care of them. Moses decided to take the sheep to a special place to find new food to eat.

Oh, my goodness! What did Moses see? High up on the mountain Moses saw a bush that was burning. The bush was burning, but it was not burning up! Moses climbed up the mountain to look at the bush. God spoke to Moses from the bush. "Moses, take off your shoes. This is holy ground." Moses did as God told him to.

Then God spoke again from the burning bush. "I am God. My people who are living in Egypt are being treated very badly. I want you to help my people. I want you to go to Egypt and bring my people back here to this special land. Go to the king of Egypt and tell him to let my people go."

Moses was surprised. He wasn't sure that he could talk to the king of Egypt. "How will I know what to do and say?" Moses asked God.

God spoke from the burning bush. "I will be with you. I will help you know what to say. When you rescue my people, you will come back to this mountain to worship me." Moses knew that God would be with him. He decided that he could go to Egypt to help the Hebrew people who lived there.

Creative Fun

Make a copy of the burning bush picture for each child. Invite the children to color the picture. Then cut the picture into five pieces to create a puzzle. Place the puzzle pieces in an envelope, one for each child. Invite the children to assemble the puzzle. Then let them glue the puzzle onto a piece of construction paper.

27

LET MY PEOPLE GO!

by Sharilyn Adair

the Bible

Exodus 4:10–12:39

God said,
"I will be with you."

(Exodus 3:12, adapted)

Supplies

crayons
markers

Bible Story

The king of Egypt was called Pharaoh. He was a bad king. He made the Hebrew people work too hard in the hot sun. God sent Moses to help the Hebrew people get away from that mean Pharaoh. God told Moses what to tell Pharaoh.

Moses said, "God says, 'Let my people go!'"

"No," said Pharaoh.

Moses went back to Pharaoh. Moses said, "God says, 'Let my people go! If you don't, I will fill your whole country with frogs. There will be frogs everywhere! You won't even be able to sit down without sitting on a frog. Let my people go!'"

"No," said Pharaoh.

So God filled the whole country with frogs that said, "Ribbit! Ribbit!"

Pharaoh still didn't let the people go. So God sent Moses back to Pharaoh several times. Each time Moses said, "God says, 'Let my people go!'" Mostly Pharaoh said no. But sometimes he would say yes and then change his mind. He was really mean.

One time God filled the whole country of Egypt with flying bugs. ZZzzz. Zzzz. But Pharaoh didn't let the Hebrew people go. Another time God made all the people who lived in Egypt get red spots all over them. But Pharaoh didn't let the Hebrew people go.

God did many other things to make Pharaoh let the Hebrew people go. Finally, Pharaoh yelled, "All right! I give up! Get those people out of here. They can take their animals and everything!"

The Hebrew people were happy. They followed Moses out of the land of Egypt. Moses was glad that he could be God's helper.

Creative Fun

Make a copy of the Bible verse poster for each child to color. Say the Bible verse with the children several times.

God said, "I will be with you."

Exodus 3:12, adapted

IN THE WILDERNESS

by Sharilyn Adair

The Bible

Exodus 16:1-31

God said,
"I will be with you."
(Exodus 3:12, adapted)

Supplies

scissors
construction
paper
crayons
markers
glue
tape

Bible Story

The Hebrew people grumbled.
"We are hungry," they all said.
"We should have stayed in Egypt,
Where at least we had some bread.

"Why did you lead us out here,
where there's not a bite to eat?
We wish we had some bread,
And just a little meat."

"Don't worry," answered Moses.
"For God knows just what we need.
And God is always with us,
So prepare yourselves to feed."

And sure enough that evening,
Quail birds flew into their camp.
They had those birds for dinner
Before the ground got damp.

And early in the morning
When the sun dried up the ground,
Some flaky, tasty white stuff
Was lying all around.

They didn't recognize it,
But it tasted good, they said.
And so they called it manna
And ate it up like bread

So that forever after
They had enough to eat,
And thanked the Lord for sending them
The manna and the meat.

Creative Fun

Make a copy of the "Bird Bonnet" for each child and cut out
the pieces. Cut two strips of construction paper for each child.
Let the children decorate the birds. Tape a headband strip to
each side of the bird to fit the bonnet to each child's head.

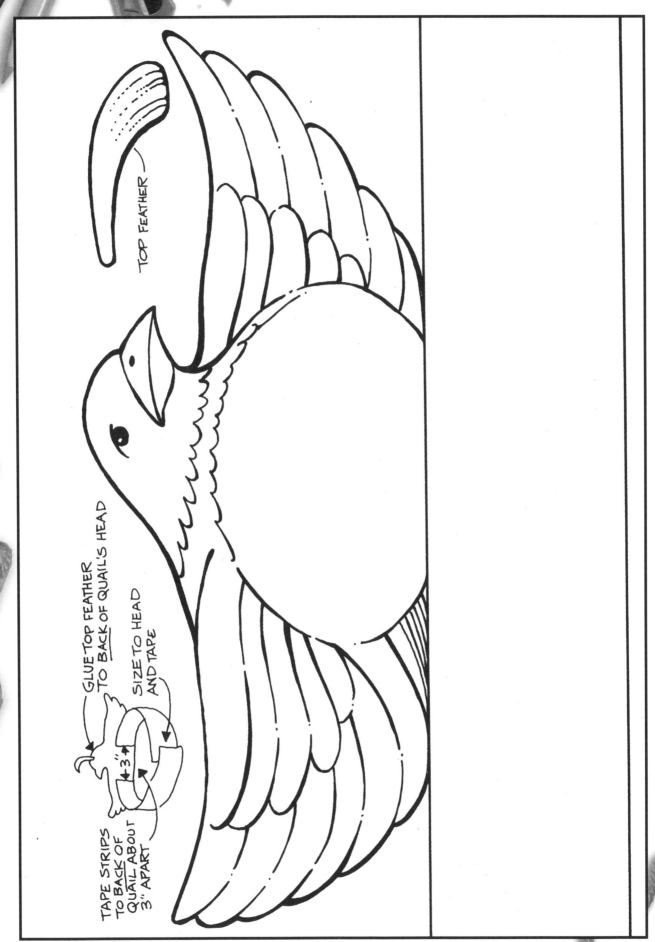

TOP FEATHER

GLUE TOP FEATHER
TO BACK OF QUAIL'S HEAD

SIZE TO HEAD
AND TAPE

3"

TAPE STRIPS
TO BACK OF
QUAIL ABOUT
3" APART

TEN COMMANDMENTS

by Elizabeth Parr

The Bible

Exodus 19:1-7; 20:1-17

God said,
"I will be with you."
(Exodus 3:12, adapted)

Supplies

crayons
markers

Bible Story

Ask the children to count with you when there is counting in the story.

1-2-3-4-5-6-7-8-9-10
God called Moses to come up high.
"Climb up to the top of Mount Sinai.
There are special rules for the people to hear.
I'll tell them to you and make them clear."

1-2-3-4-5-6-7-8-9-10
"'Love God' is one rule that I give to you.
'Love your mom and dad' is another rule too.
'Don't take things that belong to someone.'
We can follow God's rules and still have great fun.

1-2-3-4-5-6-7-8-9-10
These are rules that God gave to us.
We must obey and not make a fuss.
We should love God with all of our heart.
We should follow God's rules and all do our part.

1-2-3-4-5-6-7-8-9-10
God gave us rules to help us know
How we should live wherever we go.
The Ten Commandments that God gave Moses that day
Show that God loves us all, and we can follow God's way.

Creative Fun

Make a copy of the number puzzle for each child. Have the children use crayons or markers to make dots in each space to equal the number shown. Read each number for the children and count with the children as they make the dots. Remind the children that God gave us ten special rules to help us know how God wants us to live.

33

A HOUSE FOR GOD

by Elizabeth Parr

The Bible

Exodus 25:1-9; 35:4—36:7

Be thankful and praise the LORD as you enter his temple. (Psalm 100:4, CEV)

Supplies

scissors
crayons
markers
clear tape
shiny, curling ribbon

Creative Fun

Make a copy of the streamer handle for each child and cut them out. Let the children decorate the paper with crayons or markers. Show the children how to roll up the paper to make a tube. Tape it together. Tape pieces of shiny, curling ribbon to one end of the tube.

Bible Story

One day God told the people to build a special tent called a Tabernacle. This would be a place where the people could praise God. They could sing. They could pray. They could hear words from the Bible. The people wanted to thank God for taking care of them and loving them.

We can praise the Lord! *(Children stand, wave streamer.)*

God told the people what kind of fabric to use in the curtains. God told them what kind of wood to use. God told them to use gold to make the lampstands.

We can praise the Lord! *(Children stand, wave streamer.)*

The people were so excited to build the Tabernacle to say "thank you" to God. They wanted to give back to God because God had been so good to them. They looked forward to having a special place to pray to God.

We can praise the Lord! *(Children stand, wave streamer.)*

Everybody gave something to build the Tabernacle. They gave fabrics. They gave gold they had brought from Egypt. Everyone helped to build this special place for God.

We can praise the Lord! *(Children stand, wave streamer.)*

When the Tabernacle was finished, the people looked around. The curtains were blue, purple, and red with pictures on them. The lampstand was gold and shiny. The tables were of a special wood with gold on the tops. What a wonderful place to worship God!

We can praise the Lord! *(Children stand, wave streamer.)*

...Roll to this line...

Be thankful and praise the LORD as You enter his Temple.

Psalm 100:4

Contemporary English Version

DAVID

by Elizabeth Parr

the Bible

Psalm 23

Your kindness and love will always be with me.

(Psalm 23:6, CEV)

supplies

white glue
shallow
    containers
cotton swab
cotton balls

Bible story

David was a shepherd boy who lived a long time ago. Each day he would watch over his father's sheep. He would make sure they had water to drink. He helped the sheep find green grass too. He made sure the sheep were safe from wild animals.

Children: Baa. Baa. Baa.

David made sure that the sheep stayed on the path and didn't fall down the hill. If one of the sheep wandered off and got lost, he would find the sheep. No matter what happened, David watched out for the sheep.

Children: Baa. Baa. Baa.

When the sheep were sleeping, David was all by himself. He loved to sing songs and play his lyre. David sang songs about the wonderful world that God had made. David sang songs about God's love. David praised God by singing while the sheep slept.

Children: Baa. Baa. Baa.

One song that David sang was about God being like our shepherd. God takes care of us. God helps us to know the right way to live. God provides food and water for us. God is like a shepherd. God keeps us safe. God is always with us.

Children: Baa. Baa. Baa.

creative fun

Make a copy of the sheep on the following page. Fill shallow containers with white glue. Give each child a sheep, a cotton swab, and a stack of white cotton balls. Have the children glue the cotton balls onto the sheep. Remind them that God cares for us like a shepherd cares for his sheep.

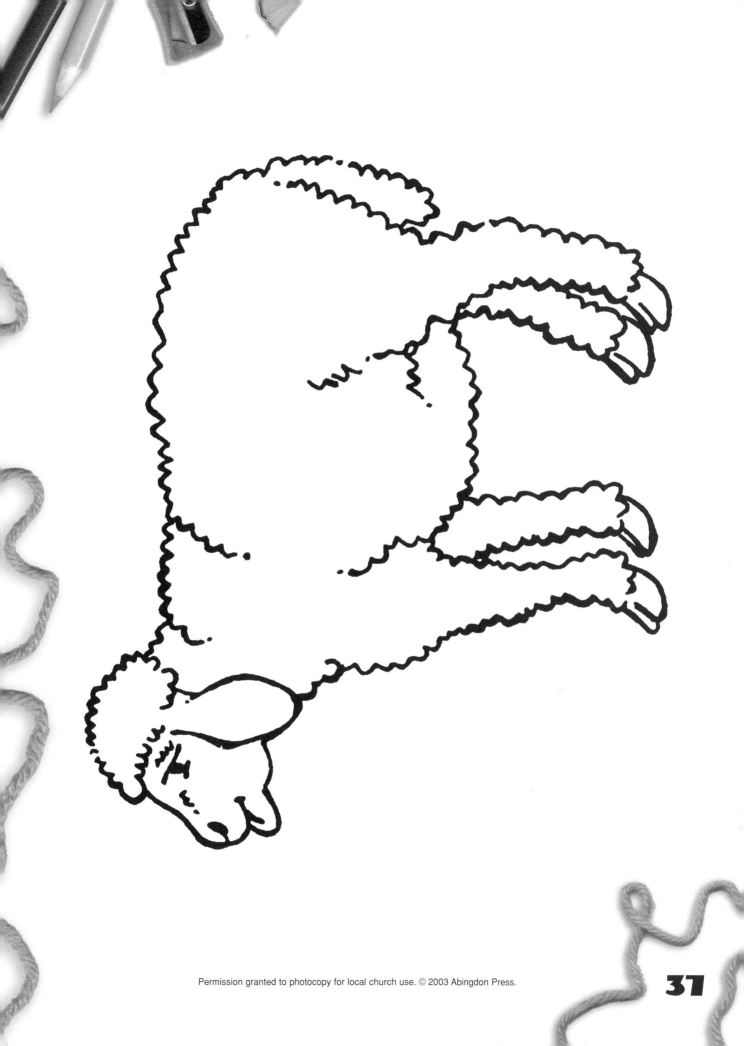

DAVID AND GOLIATH

by Elizabeth Parr

The Bible

1 Samuel 17

*I trust you
and am not afraid.*
(Psalm 56:4, CEV)

Supplies

**scissors
smooth rocks
glue
tissue paper
cotton swabs**

Bible Story

(Children stomp.) Goliath stomped his feet as he walked back and forth. Goliath was very tall, over nine feet tall. He was walking in front of King Saul's army. Goliath shouted to the people in King Saul's army. "I am the strongest soldier. I can beat anyone in your army. Who will fight with me?"

(Children shake in fear.) The men in King Saul's army were afraid of Goliath because he was so big and strong. They did not want to have to fight Goliath.

(Children run in place.) David hurried to take food to his brothers who were in King Saul's army. He was not big and strong like Goliath. But David trusted God. David knew God would take care of him. When David arrived at King Saul's camp, he heard Goliath yelling at the army. He asked some of the soldiers why no one was going to fight Goliath.

(Children motion with hand to come.) Some of the soldiers overheard David talking. They told the king what they had heard. King Saul asked David to come and see him. When King Saul saw David, he did not think David could fight Goliath. But David knew that he could fight Goliath and win. David trusted God.

(Children pretend to pick up stones.) David gathered five smooth stones in his leather bag. He went to fight Goliath. Goliath laughed at David because he was so small. But David put a stone in his sling and threw it at Goliath. Goliath fell down. David was happy that he had beaten Goliath. God was with David. David trusted God to take care of him.

Creative Fun

Make one copy of the "Trust God" circles on the following page and cut out the circles. Give each child a smooth rock. Have them use cotton swabs to paint the rock with white glue and place small pieces of tissue paper over the rock until it is covered. Then place one of the circles on the top of the rock. Paint over the circle with white glue. Set the rocks aside to dry.

39

VERY GOOD FRIENDS

by Daphna Flegal

the Bible

1 Samuel 18:1-4

A friend loves
at all times.
(Proverbs 17:17)

supplies

scissors
envelopes
glue
construction
paper
crayons
markers

Bible Story

David lived with King Saul. He became friends with King Saul's son, Jonathan.
David and Jonathan were very good friends. (Stomp, stomp, clap, clap. Stretch and bend.)

One day Jonathan wanted to give David a special gift. He gave David his robe and his belt.
David and Jonathan were very good friends. (Stomp, stomp, clap, clap. Stretch and bend.)

David knew that the robe and belt were special to Jonathan. He was happy to have Jonathan's gift. David put on the robe and belt.
David and Jonathan were very good friends. (Stomp, stomp, clap, clap. Stretch and bend.)

David and Jonathan made a promise to each other. They promised that they would always be very good friends.
David and Jonathan were very good friends. (Stomp, stomp, clap, clap. Stretch and bend.)

David and Jonathan kept their promise to one another. They helped one another. They showed love to one another.
David and Jonathan were very good friends. (Stomp, stomp, clap, clap. Stretch and bend.)

creative Fun

Make a copy of the puzzle on the following page. Cut the pieces apart on the guide lines. (Be careful not to mistake the bowstring for a guideline.) Place the pieces in an envelope. Have the children assemble the puzzle. Then glue the assembled puzzle onto construction paper. The children can then color the picture.

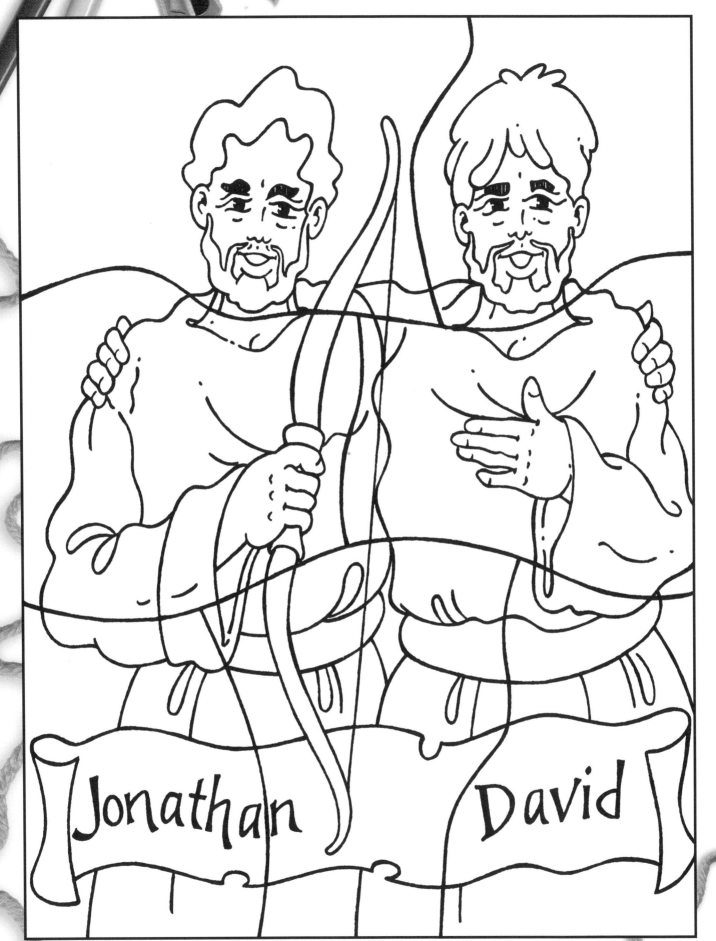

Jonathan   David

DAVID THE KING

by Elizabeth Parr

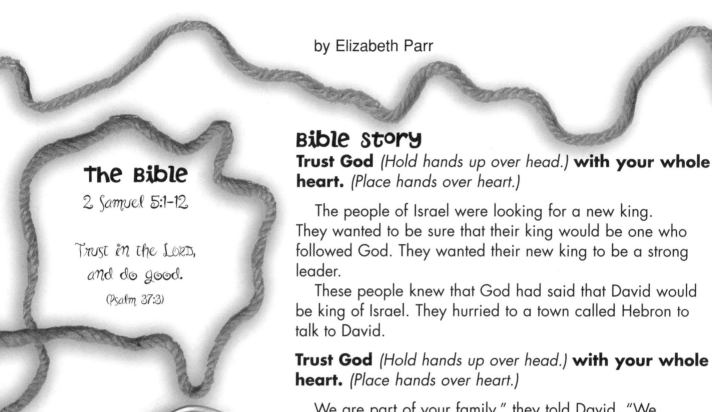

the Bible

2 Samuel 5:1-12

Trust in the LORD,
and do good.

(Psalm 37:3)

supplies

scissors
crayons
markers
glitter
glue
tape

Bible Story

Trust God *(Hold hands up over head.)* **with your whole heart.** *(Place hands over heart.)*

The people of Israel were looking for a new king. They wanted to be sure that their king would be one who followed God. They wanted their new king to be a strong leader.

These people knew that God had said that David would be king of Israel. They hurried to a town called Hebron to talk to David.

Trust God *(Hold hands up over head.)* **with your whole heart.** *(Place hands over heart.)*

We are part of your family," they told David. "We remember that you led our country in battle. We know that God promised that one day you would be our king."

David listened to all that the people had to say. He agreed to be their leader with God's help. The people poured olive oil on his head so that everyone would know that David was now king.

Trust God *(Hold hands up over head.)* **with your whole heart.** *(Place hands over heart.)*

David listened to God. David trusted God to help him be a good and strong leader for the people.

David moved to Jerusalem. He had the people rebuild the city. David became a great king because God was with him. God helped David know the right things to do.

Trust God *(Hold hands up over head.)* **with your whole heart.** *(Place hands over heart.)*

Creative Fun

Make a copy of the crown for each child in the class. Have the children decorate the crown. Then tape the pieces together and fit each child's crown to his or her head. Remind the children that David was a good king because he listened to God.

42

SOLOMON'S TEMPLE

by Sharilyn Adair

the Bible

1 Kings 6:1-22

Let the peoples praise you, O God.

(Psalm 67:3)

Supplies

**wooden blocks
metallic crayons
gold marker
pens**

Bible Story

Give each child two wooden blocks from a toy block set.

King Solomon was busy. "I have a lot of work to do," he said. "The people do not have a building where they can worship God. We need a Temple where everyone can come. I will get workers to build the Temple.

"I must find workers who can make big blocks of stone and other workers who can set them on top of each other. *(Children bang blocks together.)*

"I must find workers who can hammer wood. *(Children pound fist of one hand into palm of other hand.)* I must find workers who can carve pictures in the wood and other workers who can cover the wood with gold." *(Hold up hands and wiggle fingers.)*

So King Solomon called many workers together. He had stone cutters who knew how to cut stone into big blocks and other workers who knew how to make walls by setting the big blocks on top of each other. *(Children bang blocks together.)*

He had carpenters who knew how to hammer wood. *(Pound fists into palms.)* He had carvers who knew how to decorate the wood by carving pictures in the wood and other workers who knew how to cover the wood with gold. *(Hold up hands and wiggle fingers.)*

King Solomon said, "We need to build a Temple where people can come to worship God. You must do your best work to build a beautiful Temple."

Finally the Temple was ready. It was beautiful. The people were glad they had a place to go to worship God.

Creative Fun

Make a copy of Solomon's Temple on the following page for each child. Let the children color the Temple using metallic crayons or gold marker pens.

45

RAVENS FOR ELIJAH

by LeeDell Stickler

The Bible

1 Kings 17:1-7

God cares for you.

(1 Peter 5:7, adapted)

Supplies

scissors
crayons
markers
construction
paper
stapler
staples

Bible Story

Ahab was the king of all of Israel. He was not a good king. He was mean to the people. He did not live as God wanted him to live. *(Children stand up, fold arms across the chest, and say, "You better do right! You better do right!")*

One day God told Elijah to go to King Ahab. "Tell him that I am disappointed in him. He is being a bad king. He must change his ways." *(Children stand up, fold arms across the chest, and say, "You better do right! You better do right!")*

"If he doesn't change his ways, I am going to cause a drought. There will be no rain for weeks and weeks and weeks. All the crops will dry up. All the people and animals will be very thirsty." *(Children stand up, fold arms across the chest, and say, "You better do right! You better do right!")*

Elijah went to see King Ahab. Elijah told the king just what God had said. King Ahab was very angry with Elijah. *(Children stand up, fold arms across the chest, and say, "You better do right! You better do right!")*

Elijah was afraid of King Ahab. He knew he had to hide where the king could not find him. Elijah went to a small cave that God had told him about. A small stream ran beside the cave so that Elijah could have water. Elijah would stay here. *(Children stand up, fold arms across the chest, and say, "You better do right! You better do right!")*

While Elijah lived at the cave, God took care of him. Every morning and every evening God sent ravens to bring meat and bread to Elijah. Elijah was safe from the angry king. *(Children stand up, fold arms across the chest, and say, "You better do right! You better do right!")*

Creative Fun

Make a copy of the raven mask for each child in the class. Let the children color the mask. Attach a strip of construction paper to the back as a headband to fit the mask to each child. Remind the children that Elijah obeyed God and trusted God to take care of him.

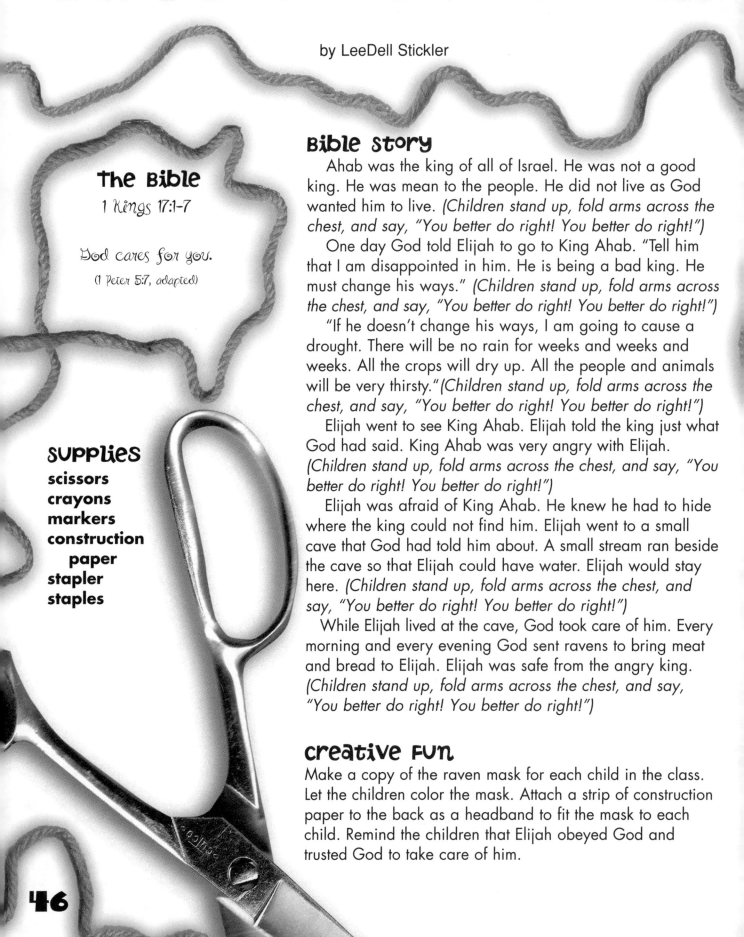

CUT OUT
PUPILS
OF EYES

THE LIONS' DEN

by Daphna Flegal

The Bible

Daniel 6:1-23, 25-28

Pray at all times.
(Romans 12:12,
Good News Translation)

Supplies

scissors
crayons
markers
yellow
   construction
   paper
glue

Bible Story

Daniel loved God. He prayed to God every day. Daniel was the king's helper. He worked very hard for the king.

But there were some men who did not like Daniel. They wanted Daniel's job as the king's helper. These men tried to make trouble for Daniel. They wanted to throw Daniel to some very hungry lions.

They tricked the king into making a new rule. The new rule said that everyone had to pray to the king, not to God. If someone did not pray to the king, he or she had to go in with the lions.

"The king is my friend," said Daniel. "but I cannot pray to the king. I pray to God."

The men watched Daniel pray to God. Then they ran to the king. "Daniel has broken your new rule," they said. "Now you must throw him to the lions."

The king was very sad. But the king had to obey the new rule. "I pray that your God will take care of you, Daniel," said the king. He put Daniel in with the lions.

The king worried all night. He kept thinking about Daniel and the lions. The next morning the king hurried to Daniel. "Daniel! Daniel!" cried the king. "Are you all right?"

"Yes," answered Daniel. "I'm fine. I prayed to God and asked God to help me." Daniel walked out of the lions' den.

"I'm happy your God kept you safe," said the king. "Now, I will make a new rule. Everyone will pray to your God." Daniel continued to pray to God every day. He knew he could talk to God and ask God to help him any time.

Creative Fun

Make a copy of the lion face for each child. Have the children cut out the face and color it. Then cut a piece of yellow construction paper into an 8-inch circle. Have the children cut from the circle's outside edge to the center (but not all the way through), making a fringe all the way around. Glue the lion face in the center of the lion's mane.

QUEEN ESTHER

by Daphna Flegal

the Bible

The Book of Esther

Love one another.
(John 15:17)

supplies
aluminum
foil
gold foil
paper
scissors
glue

Bible story

Esther was very beautiful. She was also kind and loving. She lived with her cousin. Esther and her cousin were Jews. They loved God.

One day the king decided to marry a new queen. Esther went with her cousin to the palace to meet the king. When the king met Esther, he chose her to be his new queen. She was very happy. Esther liked being the queen and living in the palace.

Haman worked for the king. He was a selfish man. Haman thought that he was more important than other people. Haman did not like the Jews. He wanted to do something to hurt the Jews. Haman tricked the king into making a law to kill all people who were Jews.

Queen Esther and her cousin were very upset. They were Jewish. "You must help our people," her cousin told Queen Esther. "You must talk to the king."

"I'm afraid," said Queen Esther. "The king might decide to kill me."

"You must be brave," said her cousin.

Queen Esther decided she would be brave. She asked her people to pray for her. Esther knew that God wanted her to help her people. Esther went to the king. Esther told him she was a Jew. Queen Esther told the king about Haman's plan to kill all the Jews.

The king was very angry. He loved Queen Esther. He did not want the Jews killed. The king ordered his men to take Haman away. Queen Esther helped her people.

Creative Fun

Make a copy of the picture of Queen Esther for each child. Have the children use aluminum foil or gold foil paper to make a special crown for Queen Esther and glue the crown onto her head.

51

NEHEMIAH'S WALL

by Sharilyn Adair

the Bible

Nehemiah 2-6

I will give thanks to the LORD with my whole heart.

(Psalm 9:1)

supplies

glue
brown, black, and gray construction paper

Bible story

"I'm so sad," said Nehemiah, "the city of Jerusalem is a mess. All the city walls have been knocked down. The people are not safe without walls around the city. I want to help."

Nehemiah went to the king. "Please, King," said Nehemiah, "let me go back to the city of Jerusalem. I want to help the people there rebuild the city walls."

"You may go," said the king. So the king let Nehemiah go to Jerusalem. The king even sent wood and building supplies to help build the wall.

When Nehemiah got to the city of Jerusalem, he talked to the people. "Listen," Nehemiah said to them, "if we all work together, we can fix our walls. God will be with us and help us."

"We can do it!" said the people. "We can fix the walls." So they started building back the walls.

Some people didn't think that the walls could be built. Some people even made fun of the workers. But that didn't stop them. Nehemiah reminded the people that God would help them. He divided the people into teams. While some people worked on the walls, others watched out to keep them safe.

Finally the wall was finished. The people were happy. "We are glad that God helped us rebuild our walls," they all said.

creative fun

Make a copy of the wall picture for each child. Give the children pieces of brown, black, and gray construction paper. Have them tear the paper into stone-shaped pieces and glue the stones onto the wall.

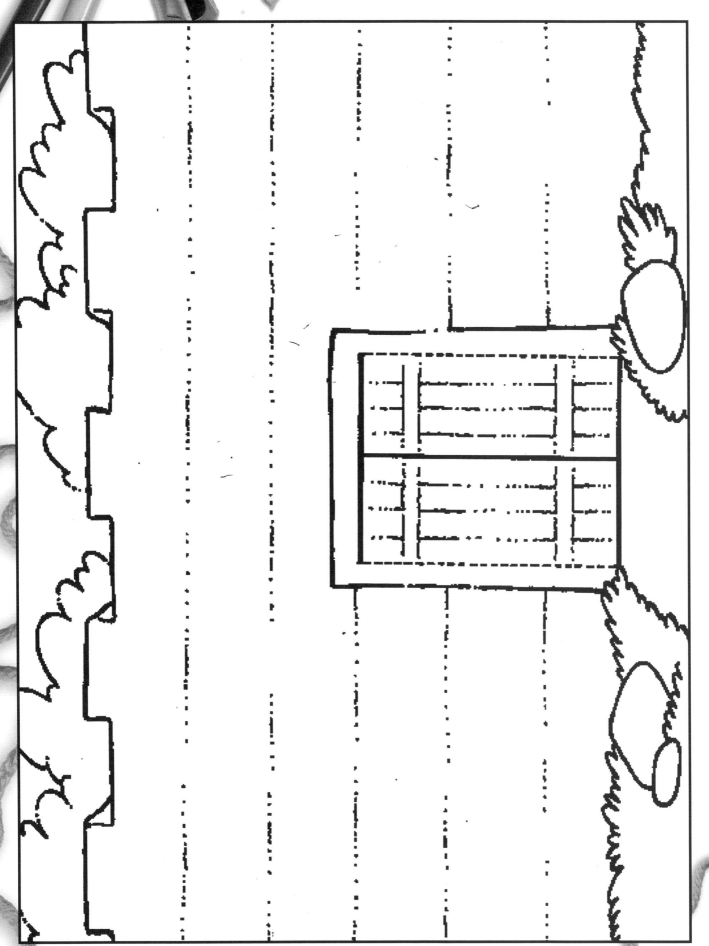

53

JONAH AND THE FISH

by Daphna Flegal

The Bible

Jonah 1:1–3:3

Pray at all times.
Romans 12:12,
Good News Translation)

Supplies

sponge
washable
tempera
paint

Bible Story

"Jonah, Jonah," said God one day. *(Point finger.)*
"Go to Nineveh, go right away." *(Point far away.)*
"No, no, no," Jonah answered that day. *(Pat hands on legs.)*
"I won't go to Nineveh; I'll run away." *(Pat hands on legs.)*
So Jonah took a ride on a great big boat. *(Rock back and forth.)*
And went to sleep while he was afloat. *(Pretend to sleep.)*
Then the wind started blowing and the waves crashed about. *(Rock back and forth.)*
"Wake up, Jonah!" the men began to shout. *(Cup hands around mouth.)*
Jonah woke up and saw the ocean waves. *(Hand over eyes.)*
"Throw me in the water so that you can be saved!" *(Pretend to dive in water.)*
The men picked up Jonah and threw him in the sea. *(Pretend to swim.)*
Where a great big fish just happened to be. *(Put palms together to make fish with hands.)*
The fish swallowed Jonah down into its belly. *(Rub stomach.)*
He stayed there three days all wet and smelly. *(Pinch nose.)*
While inside the fish, Jonah prayed and prayed. *(Fold hands in prayer.)*
God heard his prayers from where they were made. *(Cup hands around ears.)*
The fish spit Jonah out onto dry land. *(Make fish with hands. Open palms and then snap them back together.)*
Then Jonah went to Nineveh just as God planned. *(Walk in place.)*

Creative Fun

Make a copy of the Bible verse poster on the following page. Make a paint pad with a sponge and washable tempera paint. Have the children press their thumbs or fingers on the pad and then press them onto the fish to make fish scales. Let the children add as many as they choose.

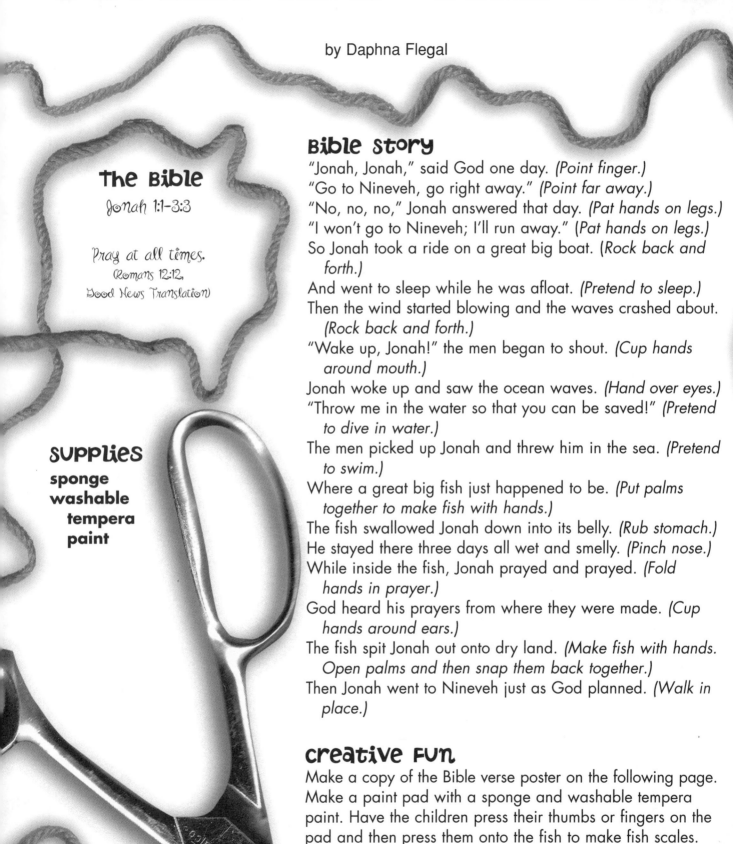

Pray
at all
times.

Romans 12:12,
Good News Translation

THE LOST SCROLLS

by Daphna Flegal

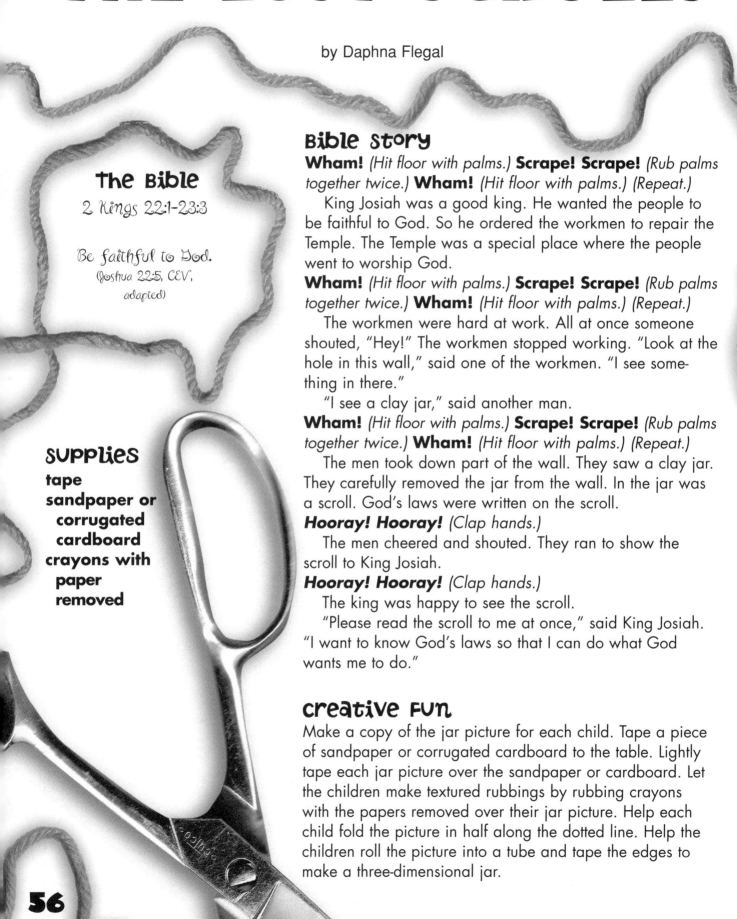

the Bible
2 Kings 22:1-23:3

Be faithful to God.
(Joshua 22:5, CEV, adapted)

supplies
tape
sandpaper or
corrugated
cardboard
crayons with
paper
removed

Bible Story

Wham! *(Hit floor with palms.)* **Scrape! Scrape!** *(Rub palms together twice.)* **Wham!** *(Hit floor with palms.) (Repeat.)*

King Josiah was a good king. He wanted the people to be faithful to God. So he ordered the workmen to repair the Temple. The Temple was a special place where the people went to worship God.

Wham! *(Hit floor with palms.)* **Scrape! Scrape!** *(Rub palms together twice.)* **Wham!** *(Hit floor with palms.) (Repeat.)*

The workmen were hard at work. All at once someone shouted, "Hey!" The workmen stopped working. "Look at the hole in this wall," said one of the workmen. "I see something in there."

"I see a clay jar," said another man.

Wham! *(Hit floor with palms.)* **Scrape! Scrape!** *(Rub palms together twice.)* **Wham!** *(Hit floor with palms.) (Repeat.)*

The men took down part of the wall. They saw a clay jar. They carefully removed the jar from the wall. In the jar was a scroll. God's laws were written on the scroll.

Hooray! Hooray! *(Clap hands.)*

The men cheered and shouted. They ran to show the scroll to King Josiah.

Hooray! Hooray! *(Clap hands.)*

The king was happy to see the scroll.

"Please read the scroll to me at once," said King Josiah. "I want to know God's laws so that I can do what God wants me to do."

creative FUN

Make a copy of the jar picture for each child. Tape a piece of sandpaper or corrugated cardboard to the table. Lightly tape each jar picture over the sandpaper or cardboard. Let the children make textured rubbings by rubbing crayons with the papers removed over their jar picture. Help each child fold the picture in half along the dotted line. Help the children roll the picture into a tube and tape the edges to make a three-dimensional jar.

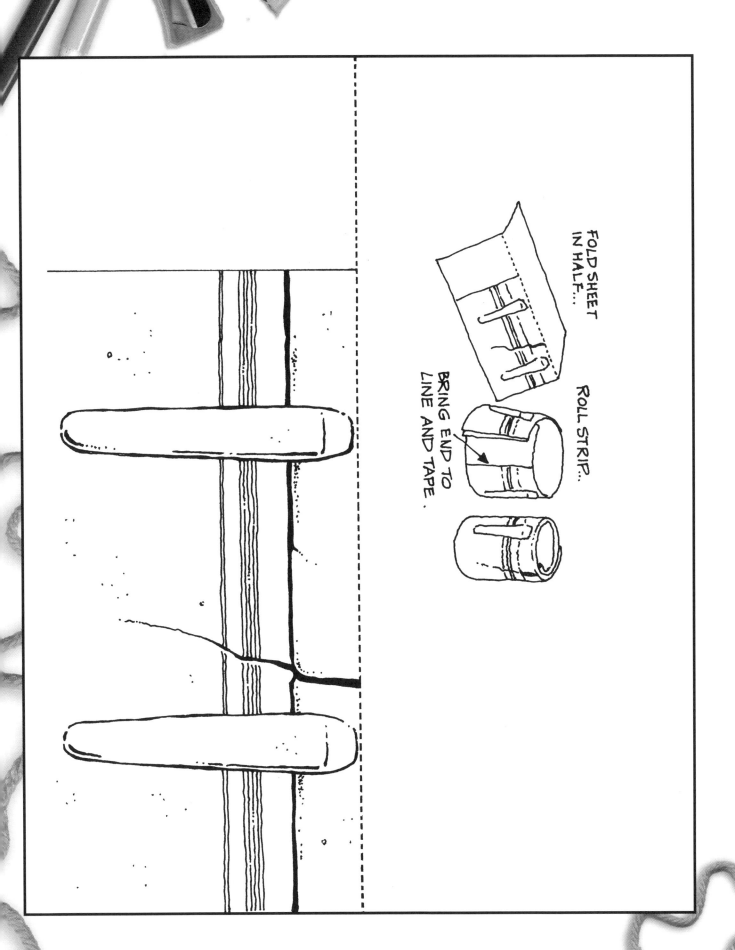

FOLD SHEET
IN HALF...

ROLL STRIP...

BRING END TO
LINE AND TAPE.

PEACEFUL KINGDOM

by Leedell Stickler

The Bible

Isaiah 11:1-7

Someone from David's family will someday be king. (Isaiah 11:1, CEV)

Supplies

scissors
tape
crayons
markers

Bible Story

Can you keep a secret? Can you keep a secret?
A new king is coming! (whisper)

He will come from the family of David.
And God will be with him.
He will be wise and kind and understanding.
He will be a different kind of king.

Can you keep a secret? Can you keep a secret?
A new king is coming! (whisper)

The new king will not judge by what he sees.
The new king will not judge by what he hears.
The new king will help the poor and the needy.
The new king will be fair in all that he does.

Can you keep a secret? Can you keep a secret?
A new king is coming! (whisper)

When the new king comes it will be wonderful!
Leopards will lie down with young goats,
and the goats won't be afraid.
Wolves will rest with the lambs,
and the lambs won't be harmed.
Cows and bears will share the same pasture.
Lions and oxen will both eat straw.

Can you keep a secret? Can you keep a secret?
A new king is coming! (whisper)

The new king will bring a time of peace.
People will know and honor the Lord.
We will live in a peaceful kingdom from that time on.

Can you keep a secret? Can you keep a secret?
A new king is coming! (whisper)

Creative Fun

Make a copy of the megaphone page for each child. Cut out the megaphone shapes. Have the children color the pictures. Tape the megaphones together. Have the children share the "secret" with one another using their megaphones.

58

GLUE TO THIS LINE

59

GOOD NEWS, MARY

by Peg Augustine

The Bible

Luke 1:26-38, 46-55

You will name him Jesus.

(Luke 1:31)

Supplies

scissors
doilies (gold or white)
glue
tape
lunch-sized paper bags
recycled newspaper or individually wrapped candies
stapler, staples

Bible Story

Mary was a young girl who lived long ago in the little town of Nazareth. Mary loved God and all the beautiful things God had made. *(Hold hands over heart.)* She liked to watch the sun come up in the morning *(Bring arms overhead forming a circle.)* and go down at night. *(Bring arms down to sides.)* She liked to look at the stars twinkling in the sky. *(Point to sky and look up.)*

One day as Mary was thinking *(Point to side of head.)* about God's beautiful world, she heard a voice. *(Cup hand around ear.)* Looking up *(Look up.)* she saw an angel standing nearby. At first Mary was surprised and frightened. *(Hold hands up in surprise.)* But the angel spoke to her in a soft voice. *(Whisper.)* "Don't be afraid, Mary. God is pleased with you. I have come to tell you a wonderful secret. *(Place finger over lips.)* God is going to send you a baby boy. And you will name him Jesus. He is God's own dear Son. *(Pretend to rock baby.)* And he is God's greatest gift to the world. He will show everyone how to help each other and how to be happy together."

Mary listened to the angel *(Cup hand around ear.)* and her heart was filled with happiness. *(Place hand over heart.)* Her own little baby *(Pretend to rock baby.)* would grow up to help other people and to show them God's love. *(Put hands over heart.)*

Each day Mary thought about God's promise to her. *(Point to side of head.)* She sang a joyful song. "My soul praises the Lord *(Raise arms above head.)* and my heart is happy." *(Put hands over heart.)*

Creative Fun

Make a copy of the angel for each child and cut them out. Glue a 6-inch white or gold doilie to the back of the angel for wings. Glue or tape the angel to the front of a lunch-sized paper bag. Stuff the bag with recycled newspaper or put individually wrapped candies in the bag. Staple the bag shut at the top. Present the bag to someone in the church.

61

JESUS IS BORN

by Judy Newman-St. John

the Bible

Luke 2:1-7

You will name him Jesus.

(Luke 1:31)

supplies

scissors
crayons
markers
tape or
 stapler and
 staples

Bible Story

Clippity clop. Clippity clop. *(Pat legs alternately.)* The gentle donkey carried Mary down the dusty, rocky road. Joseph walked beside Mary on their way to Bethlehem. They both were thinking of their baby, who would soon be born.

"You shall name him Jesus," the angel had told Mary.

Mary and Joseph knew their baby would be special. His name would be Jesus, and he would be the Son of God.

Clippity clop. Clippity clop. *(Pat legs alternately.)* The gentle donkey carried Mary down the crowded streets of Bethlehem. Joseph and Mary had gone to Bethlehem for Joseph to register. The streets were busy as people walked along the way.

Knock. Knock. *(Pretend to knock.)* "May we have a room for the night?" Joseph asked the innkeeper. "My wife is about to have a baby. We need a place to rest."

"No, no," *(Shake head no.)* said the innkeeper. "The city is so crowded with people that I have no rooms left."

Clippity clop. Clippity clop. *(Pat legs alternately.)* The gentle donkey carried Mary down the crowded street to the next inn.

Knock. Knock. *(Pretend to knock.)* "May we have a room for the night?" Joseph asked the innkeeper. "Mary is about to have a baby. We need a place to rest."

"Yes, yes," *(Nod head yes.)* said the innkeeper. "There is a stable behind the inn. It is warm, and you may rest there."

Later that night baby Jesus was born. "We love you, Jesus," Mary and Joseph said as they held their newborn baby. *(Pretend to rock baby.)*

Creative Fun

Make a copy of the donkey face for each child to decorate. Cut out the face and the strips. Help the children fold the donkeys' noses on the dotted lines. Staple the strips together for each child and fit the strips to each child's head to create a donkey hat. Staple or tape the ends of the strips together.

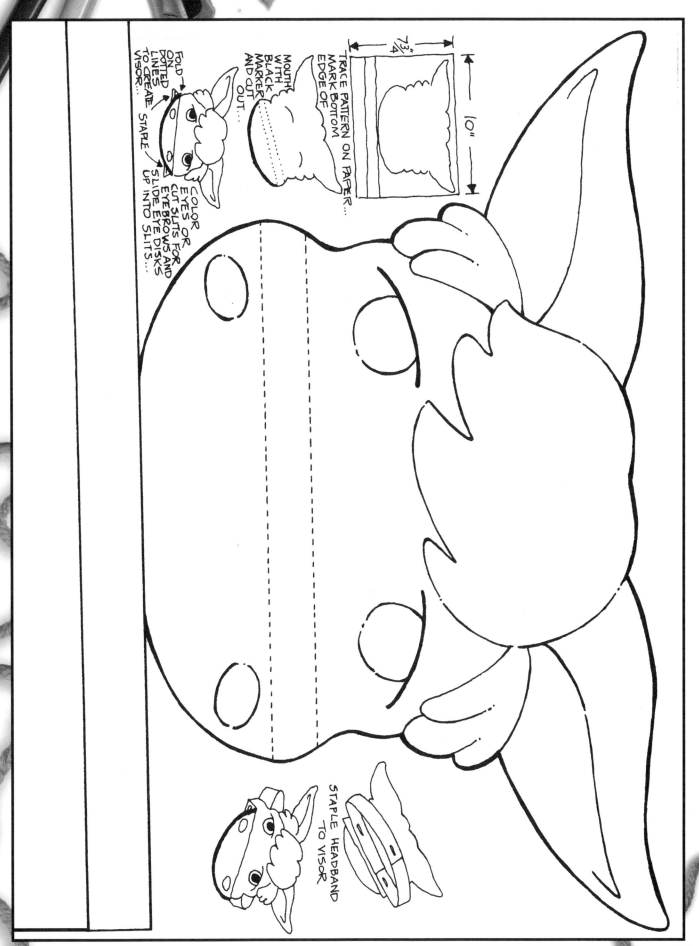

TRACE PATTERN ON PAPER...
MARK BOTTOM
EDGE OF

7¾"

10"

MOUTH
WITH
BLACK
MARKER
AND CUT
OUT...

FOLD
ON
DOTTED
LINES
TO CREATE
VISOR...

COLOR
EYES OR
CUT SLITS FOR
EYEBROWS AND
SLIDE EYE DISKS
UP INTO SLITS...
STAPLE

STAPLE HEADBAND
TO VISOR

THE SHEPHERDS

by Elizabeth Parr

The Bible

Luke 2:8-20

I am bringing you good news of great joy.

(Luke 2:10)

Supplies

crayons
markers
gel markers
or glue and
glitter

Bible Story

The shepherds were tired. They had watched over their sheep all day. Now the sheep were resting in their fold. It was a dark, dark night, and everything was very quiet.

Suddenly the sky became very bright. An angel (*Raise your hands over your head and twinkle fingers.*) appeared to the shepherds. The shepherds were frightened! "What can be happening?" they wondered. Some of the shepherds even tried to hide.

Then an angel (*Raise your hands over your head and twinkle fingers.*) said, "Do not be afraid. I am bringing you good news of great joy! A baby has been born in Bethlehem. The baby is the Son of God. He will help all people know about God's love. You will find this baby in a stable. He will be lying in a manger on a bed of hay."

When the angel (*Raise your hands over your head and twinkle fingers.*) finished speaking, the sky became even brighter as more angels appeared. The angels sang a beautiful song praising God.

When the angels left and the sky became dark again, the shepherds began to talk. Finally they said, "Let's go to Bethlehem to see if we can find this baby."

They hurried to Bethlehem. It was true! They found the stable and saw baby Jesus lying on a bed of hay. They told Mary and Joseph everything that the angels had said.

When the shepherds left to take care of their sheep, they told everyone about Jesus, who was God's Son. Everything had happened just as the angels (*Raise your hands over your head and twinkle fingers.*) had said. Baby Jesus was born!

Creative Fun

Make a copy of the shepherds picture for each child. Have the children color the picture to make the sky look like nighttime. Then have the children use gel markers to draw angels in the sky, or have them use glue and glitter to create angels.

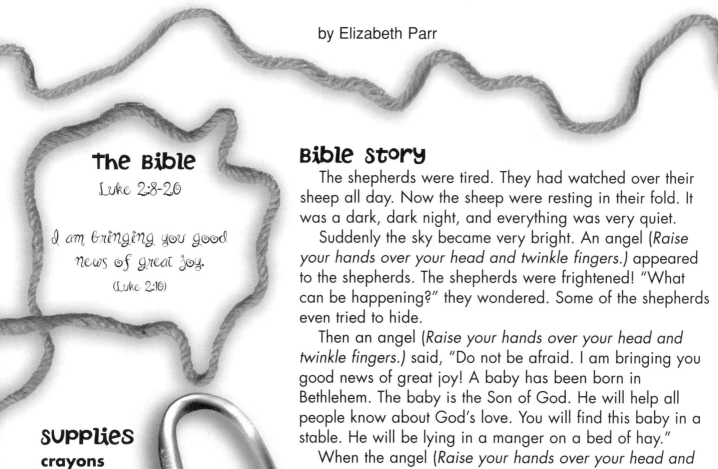

65

THE WISE MEN

by Judy Newman-St. John

the Bible

Matthew 2:1-12

We saw his star in the east and have come to worship him.
(Matthew 2:2, CEV)

supplies

scissors
crayons
markers
newspaper
masking tape
brown paper lunch bags
yarn
tape or glue

Creative Fun

Make a copy of the camel's face for each child and cut them out. Have the children color the faces. Give each child three or four double sheets of newspaper. Lay these out flat on top of each other. Help each child to roll the newspaper from the bottom right corner diagonally to the top left-hand corner. Let the child help you wrap masking tape around the newspaper to create the "body" of the camel to ride on. Stuff newspaper into brown paper lunch bags and tie the lunch bag onto one end of the newspaper body. Tape or glue the camel's face onto the bag. Help each child tape yarn reins on either side of the head.

Bible Story

One day some wise men came to Jerusalem. "Where is the special baby that has been born?" they asked the king. "We saw his star in the east and have come to worship him."

"Go to Bethlehem and find this child," King Herod said. "Come back and tell me where he is so I can worship him, too."

So the wise men got on their camels. *(Have the children ride on their paper bag camels.)* Harump! Harump! The wise men rode their camels down the road. Harump! Harump! The wise men rode their camels up the hill. Harump! Harump! The wise men rode their camels through the countryside.

The wise men saw a large, bright star in the sky. The wise men rode their camels and followed the star. Harump! Harump! The star led them to the place where Jesus was.

The wise men climbed down from their camels. *(Have the children get off their paper bag camels and put them aside.)* When the wise men stepped into the house, they saw Jesus and his mother, Mary. Quickly they got down on their knees to worship Jesus.

The wise men gave Jesus the special gifts they had brought him, gifts fit for a king. They gave him gold, frankincense, and myrrh. The wise men knew Jesus was the Son of God.

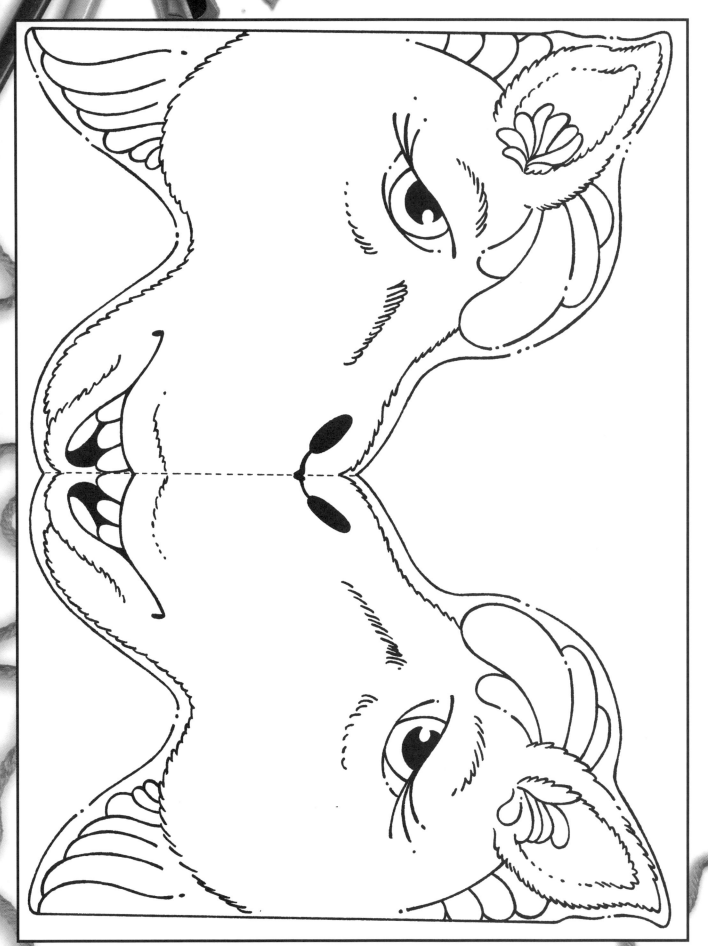

67

JESUS IN THE TEMPLE

by Peg Augustine

The Bible

Luke 2:41-52

Jesus grew both in body and in wisdom.
(Luke 2:52, Good News Translation)

Supplies

markers
crayons

Bible Story

Jesus and his family walked the long road to Jerusalem with a lot of other people. Jesus was happy that he was twelve years old and could go with his parents on their yearly trip to the Temple to worship God.

Finally they reached the city. For several days they went to worship in the Temple. All too soon it was time to go home. Mary and Joseph walked with the crowd of people back to Nazareth. They thought Jesus was walking with his friends.

When it was time to rest for the night, Mary and Joseph looked for Jesus, but they could not find him. Leaving the crowd, Mary and Joseph walked back to Jerusalem to find Jesus.

First they looked for Jesus where the boys played ball in the marketplace. Do you think Jesus was playing ball in the marketplace? **No, Jesus was not in the marketplace.** *(Shake head no.)* Next they looked for Jesus where the baker was putting bread into the big clay oven. Do you think Jesus was at the baker's? **No, Jesus was not at the baker's.** *(Shake head no.)* They looked for Jesus where the women were getting water from the well. Do you think Jesus was at the well? **No, Jesus was not at the well.** *(Shake head no.)* Finally Mary and Joseph looked at the Temple. They knew Jesus loved being at the Temple. Do you think Jesus was at the Temple? **Yes, Jesus was at the Temple.** *(Nod head yes.)*

Mary and Joseph found Jesus sitting with the Temple leaders, listening and asking questions. Jesus explained to his parents, "I thought you would know where I was. My heart is filled with love for God, and I want to learn more about God."

Mary and Joseph thought about how much they loved Jesus as they walked home with their son.

Creative Fun

Make a copy of the Temple for each child to color with gold crayons or markers. Have the children draw a picture of Jesus when he was a boy standing in the doorway of the Temple.

69

JESUS IS BAPTIZED

by Peg Augustine

The Bible

Matthew 3:13-17

"This is my own dear Son, with whom I am pleased."
(Matthew 3:17, Good News Translation)

Supplies

crayons
watercolor
  markers
pan of water
newspaper

Bible Story

Jesus walked down the hot roads of the countryside. He was looking for John. "Have you seen a man known as John the Baptizer?" Jesus asked the people he met.

"It would be harder not to hear about John," one man said. "Most of us have heard him preach. He tells us that when we say we are sorry for the things we do wrong, we must do more. We must change our hearts and lives."

"I want to hear him," Jesus said. "I want to spend some time talking to him and listening to what he says about God."

"Go to the Jordan River," the man said. "John baptizes people in the river to show that they are ready to wash away their old ways and change their hearts."

Jesus walked on. Finally he saw a huge crowd in the distance. As he got closer, he heard John's voice. "Yes," John was saying, "I baptize you with water to show that your hearts and lives have been changed. But another man will be coming soon. You must listen to him. He is much greater than I am. He will baptize you with the Spirit of God."

Jesus walked around the edge of the crowd. Then he stepped down into the cool river and waded toward John. Jesus wanted John to baptize him.

"No," John said, "why do you come to me to be baptized? I should be baptized by you!"

"I want you to baptize me," Jesus answered. "It is the right thing to do."

John agreed to baptize Jesus. Jesus felt the cool water swirling around him. Then Jesus looked up into the sky. He saw God's Spirit coming down like a dove. Then Jesus heard God's voice, "This is my own dear Son, with whom I am pleased."

Creative Fun

Make a copy of the baptism picture for each child to color with crayons. Have them use watercolor markers to add colors to the river. Help each child dip the picture into a pan of water. The water will make the markers run and have a watery effect. Set the pictures flat on newspaper to dry.

71

FOLLOW ME

by Daphna Flegal

The Bible

Luke 5:1-11;
Mark 1:16-20

And Jesus said to them,
"Follow me."

(Mark 1:17)

Supplies

crayons
blue tempera
paint
shallow trays
yarn
scissors

Bible Story

Splash. Splash. Splash. The waves splashed to the shore. Jesus was standing beside the sea. Many, many people were crowding around him. Many, many people wanted to hear Jesus tell the good news about God's love. *Splash. Splash. Splash.* The waves splashed against two boats on the sand by the sea. Fisherman Peter and his friends were beside the boats, washing their nets. *Splash. Splash. Splash.* The waves splashed as Jesus stepped into Peter's boat. He asked Peter to take the boat out onto the lake. Jesus taught the many, many people from the boat. He told the people the good news about God's love. *Splash. Splash. Splash.* The waves splashed as they rocked the boat back and forth in the water.

"Take the boat farther out," Jesus said to Peter. "Put your nets into the deep water, and you will catch some fish."

"We have fished all night," said Peter. "We did not catch any fish at all. But we can put out our nets and try again."

Splash. Splash. Splash. The waves splashed as fisherman Peter put his nets into the water. *Splash. Splash. Splash.* The waves splashed as the fish swam into the net. *Splash. Splash. Splash.* Peter called his friends to come and help him. There were so many fish that the boats began to sink! *Splash. Splash. Splash.* The waves splashed against the boats as the fishermen rowed back to shore.

"Come, follow me," said Jesus to the fishermen. "I want you to fish for people. I want you to help me tell others the good news about God's love."

Creative Fun

Make a copy of the picture for each child to color with crayons. Pour blue tempera paint into shallow trays. Cut yarn into 8-inch lengths. Show the children how to dip the yarn into the paint and then pull the yarn over their pictures to make wavy lines over the water part of the picture.

MATTHEW

by Sharilyn Adair

the Bible

Matthew 9:9-13

Jesus said, "Follow me."
(Matthew 9:9, adapted)

Supplies

coins
tape
crayons

Bible Story

Before the story, give each child four pennies. Explain that the children will count the money with you during the story.

One...two...three...four.... *(Drop four coins, one at a time, into a pile in front of you.)* Matthew was counting his money. He had collected a lot of taxes that day. *(Pick up the coins and drop them again as you count.)* Five...six... seven...eight. Matthew was a busy tax collector.

Nobody in the whole country liked tax collectors. Tax collectors took people's money and gave it to their enemies, the Romans. *(Pick up the coins.)* Matthew worked for the Romans. He knew that many people did not like him. He counted some more money: one...two...three...four. *(Drop four coins, one at a time, into a pile in front of you.)*

Then Matthew heard someone calling to him. He looked up and saw Jesus. "Follow me," said Jesus.

Matthew left his money and went with Jesus. They went to Matthew's house for dinner. Matthew invited other tax collectors and people that nobody liked.

Some men called Pharisees came by and saw Jesus eating with the people nobody liked. "Why is Jesus eating with those people?" they asked. "Nobody likes them."

Jesus answered, "I have come to show God's love for everybody, even tax collectors."

Creative Fun

Make a copy of the Bible verse poster for each child. Use a loop of tape to secure three or four coins to the table. Lightly tape the Bible verse over the coins. Show the children how to use the sides of the crayons (with papers removed) to rub over the coins. A rubbing of the coins will show on the papers.

"Follow me."

Matthew 9:9

JESUS PRAYS

by Judy Newman-St. John

The Bible

Matthew 6:9-15

Teach us to pray.

(Luke 11:1)

Supplies
multicultural crayons or markers pen or pencil

Bible Story

Jesus' friends had heard Jesus pray many times. "Dear God, thank you for this food," Jesus prayed before they shared a meal together. *(Fold hands in prayer.)* "Dear God, help me make this man well," Jesus prayed before he healed a man who could not see. *(Fold hands in prayer.)* "Dear God, help me to do what you want me to do," Jesus prayed in the garden. *(Fold hands in prayer.)*

Jesus' friends knew that every time Jesus taught the people or helped someone, Jesus prayed to God. *(Fold hands in prayer.)* Jesus' friends loved him, and they wanted to be like him.

"Teach us to pray," Jesus' friends said to him.

Jesus was happy his friends wanted to learn how to pray. He knew that prayer was a special way to talk with God. So Jesus gave his friends a special prayer to say.

"Pray this way," Jesus said. *(Fold hands in prayer.)*

Our Father in heaven,
*   hallowed be your name,*
*   your kingdom come,*
*   your will be done, on earth as in heaven.*
Give us today our daily bread.
Forgive us our sins
*   as we forgive those who sin against us.*
Save us from the time of trial,
*   and deliver us from evil,*
For the kingdom, the power, and the glory are yours
*   now and for ever. Amen.*

English translation of The Lord's Prayer by the International Consultation on English Texts. From The United Methodist Hymnal, *894.*

Creative Fun

Make a copy of the praying hands for each child. Have the children use multicultural crayons or markers to color the hands to look like their own. Help each child write a simple prayer on the page.

77

JAIRUS'S DAUGHTER

by Anita Edlund

the Bible

Matthew 9:18-19, 23-26

Sing praise to the Lord;
tell the wonderful things
God has done.
(Psalm 105:2, Good News
Translation, adapted)

Supplies
crayons
markers
tape

Bible Story

Waiting, waiting, waiting! *(Have the children stand with their arms crossed and tapping one foot.)*

A crowd of people was waiting for Jesus. They knew he was coming, and they wanted to see him.

There was a man named Jairus who really wanted to see Jesus. His daughter was very sick. He was very sad.

Kneeling, kneeling, kneeling! *(Have the children kneel on their knees.)*

When Jairus saw Jesus, he knelt down in front of him. "Please, please, come to my house," he begged. "My little girl is very sick."

Jesus went with Jairus to his house. He was going to help the little girl.

Crying, crying, crying! *(Have the children rub their eyes as if they are crying.)*

When they got to Jairus' house, the people were crying. The little girl was very sick. Jesus took a few of his helpers in the little girl's room. He took her parents with him, too. "Child, get up," Jesus said with a kind voice.

Smiling, smiling, smiling! *(Have the children smile.)*

The little girl stood up. She was well! Jesus told her parents to give her something to eat. Jesus had helped the little girl and made her well.

Creative Fun

Make a copy of the Jairus puppet for each child to decorate with crayons or markers. Fold it on the dotted line. Tape the top and side of each puppet together, leaving the bottom open. Show the children how to place their hand inside the puppet and turn the puppet to show each face. Tell the story again, without motions, and have the children use the puppet to show how Jairus was feeling at each part of the story.

THE BOY'S LUNCH

by Daphna Flegal

the Bible

Matthew 14:13-21;
John 6:1-14

God cares for you.
(1 Peter 5:7, adapted)

supplies

scissors
crayons
markers

Bible story

Five loaves of bread *(Hold up five fingers.)*
And two little fish. *(Hold up two fingers.)*
My, oh my, what a tasty dish! *(Rub stomach.)*

Five thousand people came from far and near,
To see the man Jesus, God's Son so dear.
They sat on the hillside and listened all day
To the wonderful things Jesus had to say.

Five loaves of bread *(Hold up five fingers.)*
And two little fish. *(Hold up two fingers.)*
My, oh my, what a tasty dish! *(Rub stomach.)*

They sat so long, it began to grow dark.
They became so hungry, they would eat a shark!
But when Jesus' friends took a look around
A small boy's lunch was the food they found.

Five loaves of bread *(Hold up five fingers.)*
And two little fish. *(Hold up two fingers.)*
My, oh my, what a tasty dish! *(Rub stomach.)*

The boy was happy to share his lunch,
Though he didn't think it would feed this bunch.
But Jesus took the food and then calmly said,
"Thank you, God, for this fish and bread."

Five loaves of bread *(Hold up five fingers.)*
And two little fish. *(Hold up two fingers.)*
My, oh my, what a tasty dish! *(Rub stomach.)*

Five loaves and two fish fed everyone there,
And they ate and they ate without a care.
They gathered the leftovers—twelve baskets when done.
They knew Jesus loved them each and every one.

Five loaves of bread *(Hold up five fingers.)*
And two little fish. *(Hold up two fingers.)*
My, oh my, what a tasty dish! *(Rub stomach.)*

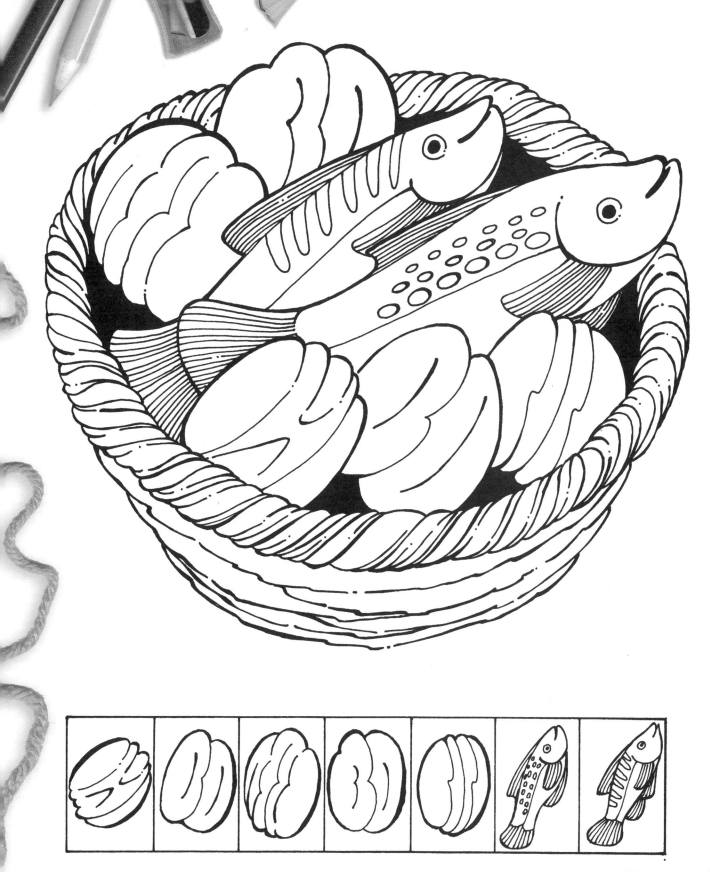

creative FUN

Make a copy of this page for each child. Cut the small pictures apart. Encourage the children to match the small pictures to the pictures in the basket. Then let the children use crayons or markers to decorate the basket of bread and fish.

81

THE LOST SHEEP

by Daphna Flegal

The Bible

Luke 15:3-7

God cares for you.
(1 Peter 5:7, adapted)

Supplies

scissors
crayons
glue
cotton balls
construction
  paper
tape

Bible Story

Jesus told a story about a shepherd and his sheep. The shepherd took care of his sheep. The shepherd took the sheep to the hillside to eat the sweet-tasting grass. While the sheep were eating, the shepherd counted his sheep. Ninety-eight. Ninety-nine. One hundred.

The shepherd took his sheep to drink water from the stream. While the sheep were drinking, the shepherd counted his sheep. Ninety-eight. Ninety-nine. One hundred.

The shepherd took his sheep to rest under a tree. While the sheep were resting, the shepherd counted his sheep. Ninety-eight. Ninety-nine. Ninety-eight. Ninety-nine! One sheep was missing! The shepherd went to look for his sheep.

One little sheep wandered off. **"Baa, baa."** First the little sheep played in the cool water of the stream. Then the little sheep was hungry. **"Baa, baa."** He ate some of the sweet-tasting grass. Then the little sheep decided it was time to take a nap. **"Baa, baa."** He rested underneath the branches of the tree.

While the little sheep was napping, a loud noise startled the little sheep. The sheep was afraid! What if the noise was a wolf or a bear? **"Baa, baa."** The little sheep ran to hide behind a rock. The little sheep was still afraid. He wished he had not wandered away from his shepherd.

The little sheep ran to a nearby bush. His wool caught on the branches of the bush. **"Baa, baa!"** cried the little sheep. The little sheep was stuck.

The shepherd heard the little sheep crying. He found the little sheep in the bush. He carefully untangled the little sheep's wool from the bush. He picked the sheep up in his arms and carried him back to the other sheep.

"Baa, baa." The little sheep was happy to be with his shepherd. Ninety-eight. Ninety-nine. One hundred! The shepherd counted his sheep. The shepherd was happy that he had found the little lost sheep.

CREATIVE FUN

Make a copy of the sheep mask for each child and cut out the eyes. Let the children decorate the masks by coloring them with crayons or by gluing on cotton balls. Cut a two-inch wide strip of construction paper for each child. Tape the strip to one side of the mask. Have the child hold the mask up to his or her face while you fit the strip around the child's head and tape it to the other side of the mask.

THE GOOD NEIGHBOR

by Daphna Flegal

the Bible

Luke 10:25-37

Love your neighbor
as yourself.
(Luke 10:27, adapted)

supplies

scissors
markers
crayons
craft sticks
tape

Bible story

Jesus told the people this story. Once there was a man traveling down the road to a town called Jericho. Suddenly robbers jumped out from behind some rocks. The robbers hurt the man and took all the man's money. Then the robbers left the man and ran away.

Soon a priest came walking down the road. He saw the hurt man lying beside the road. He knew that the man needed help, but he was afraid. He looked around to see if the robbers were still hiding nearby. The priest crossed the road and hurried by the hurt man. He did not stop to help.

Later another leader from the Temple came walking down the road. He saw the hurt man lying beside the road, but he did not want to touch the man. He crossed the road and hurried by the hurt man. He did not stop to help.

Then a third man came riding down the road on his donkey. He was called a Samaritan. He saw the hurt man lying on the road and stopped to help him. He put the hurt man on his donkey and took him to a place where he could rest and get better. The Samaritan even paid for the hurt man's care.

Jesus finished the story and looked at the people. "Three men saw the hurt man on the road," Jesus said. "Who was the neighbor to the man who was hurt?"

creative fun

Make a copy of the figures on the next page and cut them out. Let the children decorate the figures with markers or crayons. Help the children tape the figures to craft sticks to create storytelling puppets. Give each child a puppet. Have the children use the puppets to help you retell the story.

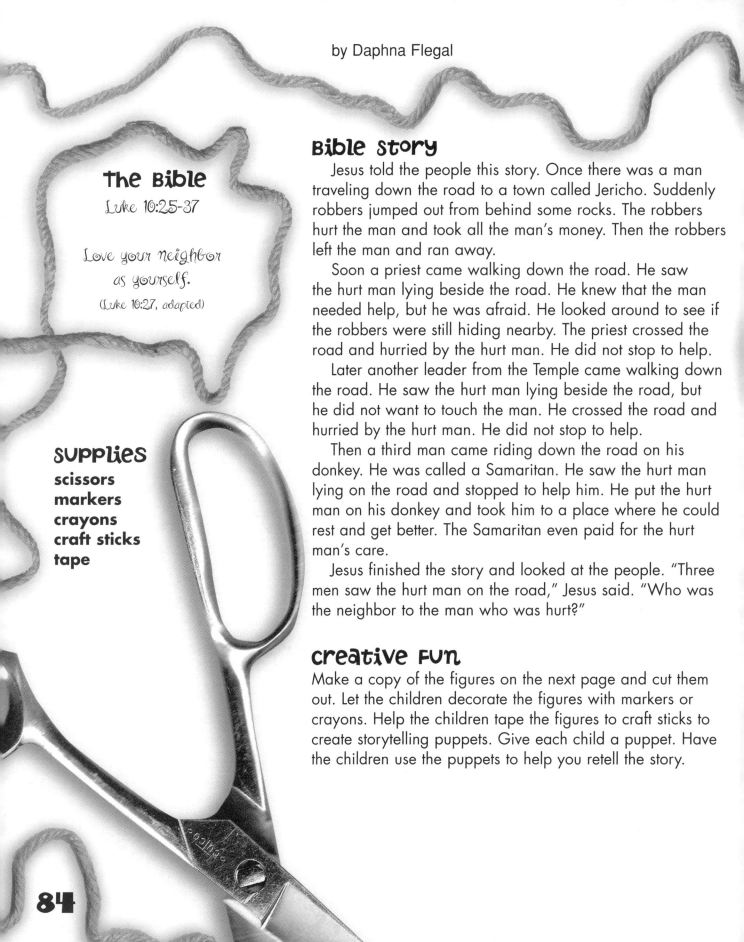

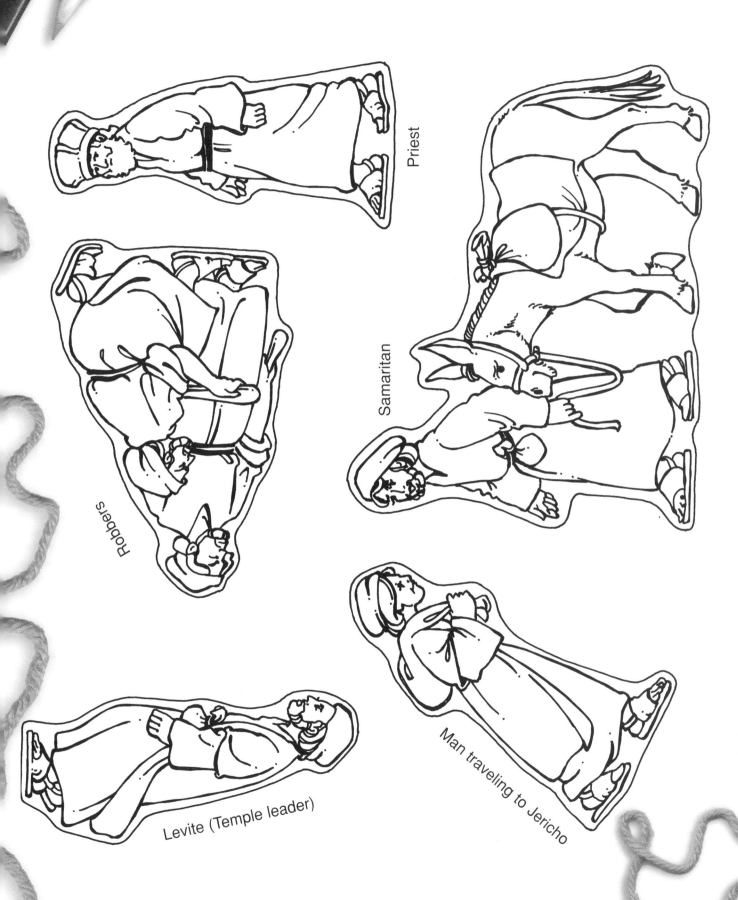

Priest

Samaritan

Robbers

Levite (Temple leader)

Man traveling to Jericho

TWO HOUSES

by Daphna Flegal

THE BIBLE

Matthew 7:24-27

God is love.

(1 John 4:8)

SUPPLIES

crayons
markers
scissors
stapler and
staples

CREATIVE FUN

Make a copy of the pictures on the next page. Have the children decorate the pictures using crayons or markers. Cut the pictures apart for each child and put them in the correct order. Staple one side of the pictures to create a storybook.

BIBLE STORY

Jesus told a story about two houses. *(Turn to the first page of the storybook.)* The wise man built his house on rock. *(Have the children put a finger on the picture of the house.)* Point to the picture of the rock. *(Have the children put a finger on the picture of the rock. Then have the children turn to the second page of their storybooks.)* One day it began to rain. It rained and rained. It rained so hard that there were floods all around the house. The winds began to blow. The water from the rains and the flood beat upon the house. Let's make the sound of the wind and rain. *(Have the children put their storybooks down. Show them how to rub their palms together to make the sound of rain. Have the children blow to make the sound of the wind.)* But the house did not fall because it had been built on rock.

(Have the children turn to the third page of their storybooks.) The foolish man built his house on sand. Point to the picture of the house. *(Have the children put a finger on the picture of the house.)* Now point to the sand. *(Have the children put a finger on the picture of sand. Then have the children turn to the fourth page of their storybooks.)* One day it began to rain. It rained and rained. It rained so hard that there were floods all around the house. The winds began to blow. The water from the rains and the flood beat upon the house. Let's make the sound of the wind and rain. *(Have the children put their storybooks down. Have them rub their palms together to make the sound of rain and blow to make the sound of the wind.)* The house built on the sand FELL DOWN! *(Slap hands on floor.)*

Jesus told this story to help people learn about God's love. When we show people God's love, we are like the wise man who built his house on the rock.

86

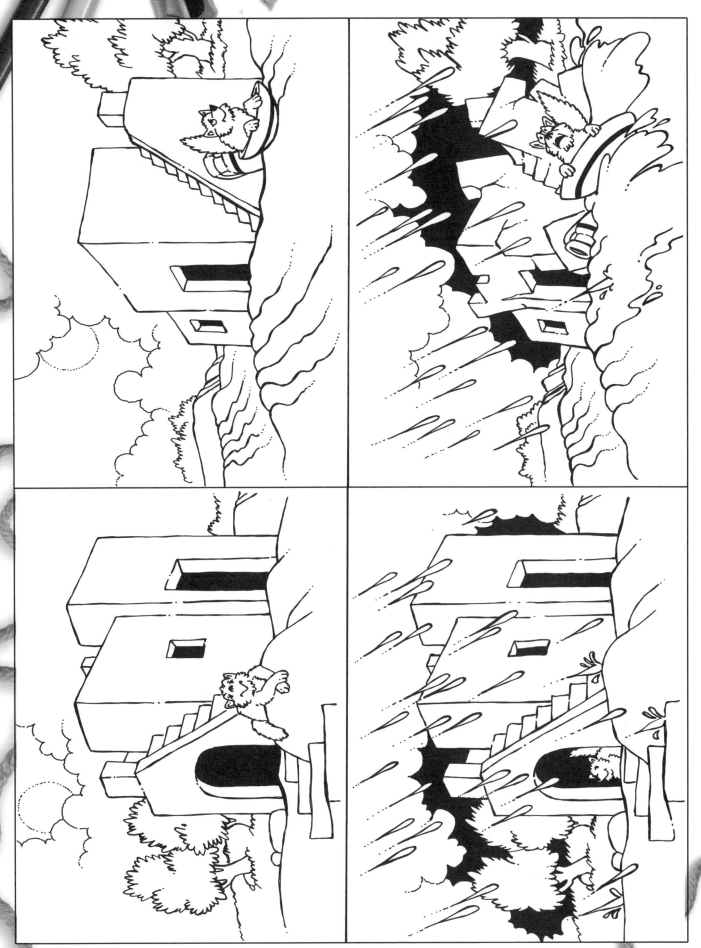

87

A LOVING FATHER

by Judy Newman-St. John

Bible Verse

Luke 15:11-32

Forgive one another.
(Ephesians 4:32,
Good News Translation)

Supplies

scissors
markers
crayons
glue

Bible Story

Jesus told this story so that people would know that God loves us and forgives us when we make mistakes.

There was a man who had two sons. He loved both of his sons very much. One day the younger son said, "Father, I am tired of living at home. Give me my share of the money you have for us."

The father was very unhappy that his son wanted to leave home, but he said nothing. He gave his younger son his share of the money.

The son went to a country far away. At first he was happy. He enjoyed spending the money he had. But soon all the money was gone. The son began to get hungry, but he could not buy any food.

"I'll get a job," decided the son. He took the job of feeding pigs. He was so hungry that he would have been glad to eat the pigs' food.

"What am I doing?" the son thought one day as he fed the pigs. He knew that his father had always taken good care of him. He decided to go home. He decided to tell his father he was sorry.

The son started the long trip home. He was still far from home when his father saw him. The father ran to his son and hugged and kissed him. "My son is home!" his father said.

The father was happy that his son had come home. He gave his son a beautiful ring and robe to wear. Then he planned a special party to celebrate his son's return. The father and son were happy to be together again.

Creative Fun

Make a copy of the card for each child. Cut the Bible verse from the bottom of the card. Cut along the solid lines around the cat and mouse. Let the children decorate the card. Help the children turn the card over and glue the Bible verse strip onto the blank side. Turn the card back over. Show the children how to fold the card to make it look like the cat and mouse are hugging each other.

Forgive one another.

Ephesians 4:32, Good News Translation

GREAT COMMANDMENT

by Elizabeth Parr

the Bible

Matthew 22:35-40

Love the Lord your God
with all your heart.
(Matthew 22:37)

Supplies

scissors
crayons
markers

Bible Story

Jesus was talking with some of the leaders one day. A teacher came up to him. He wanted to talk to Jesus. He knew Jesus could give him some answers.

"Jesus," the man said, "I have a question for you. Could you tell me what is the most important rule?"

Jesus smiled at the man. He quickly said, "We worship only one God. You should love God with all your heart, with all your soul, with all your mind, and with all your strength."

**Love God, love God, all ye little children.
God is love. God is love.**

The teacher was glad to hear what Jesus had to say. The teacher said to Jesus, "You are right. There is only one God. Loving God is more important than anything else we can do. In all that we do, we must love God."

**Love God, love God, all ye little children.
God is love. God is love.**

As Jesus listened, he knew that the man understood the importance of loving God. He knew the teacher loved God with all his heart. That is God's greatest rule.

**Love God, love God, all ye little children.
God is love. God is love.**

creative Fun

Make a copy of the heart cards for each child and cut them apart. Let the children enjoy decorating them. Then ask the children to sort the cards by size and line them up from smallest to largest. Remind the children that our verse today is "Love the Lord your God with all your heart."

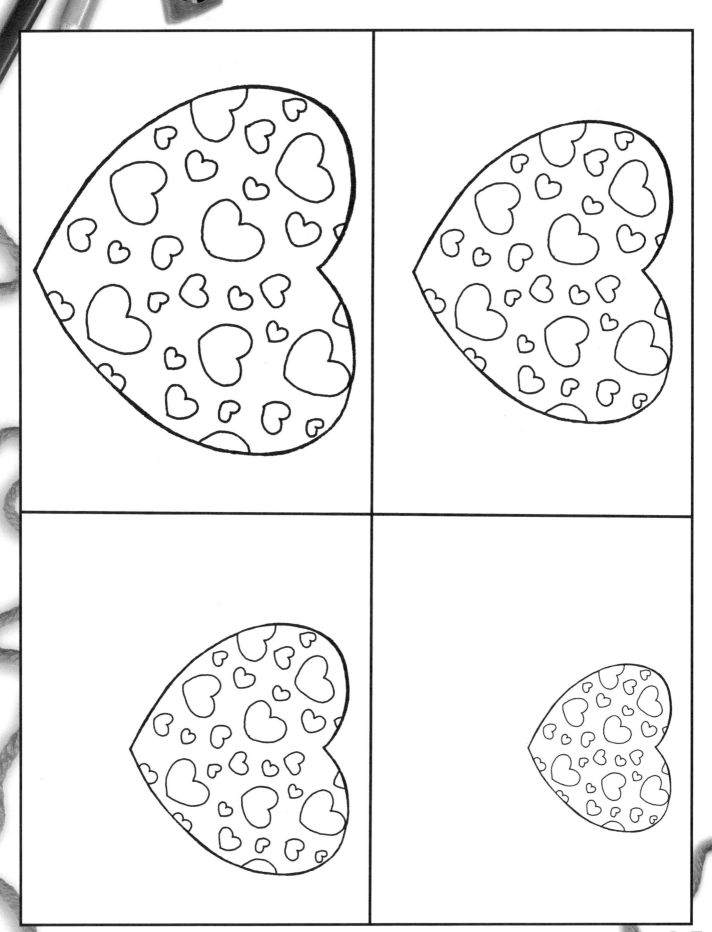

JESUS AND THE CHILDREN

by Daphna Flegal

The Bible

Mark 10:13-16

Let the little children
come to me.
(Mark 10:14)

Supplies

markers
glue
lace
glitter
tissue paper

Bible Story

"Jesus is here!" said the people in the villages, the cities, and the countryside. They hurried to where Jesus was teaching. Soon there was a crowd of people listening to Jesus. They wanted to hear what Jesus had to say about God. They all knew that Jesus loved them.

Yes, Jesus loves me!

"Jesus is here!" said the mothers holding their babies, and the fathers walking with their sons and daughters. They hurried to bring their children to see Jesus. They wanted Jesus to touch their children. They all knew that Jesus loved their children.

Yes, Jesus loves me!

"Stop!" said the men standing near Jesus. "Do not bring your children to see Jesus! Jesus does not have time for children. Take your children home." These men did not understand that Jesus loved grownups and children. Jesus loved men and women, boys and girls, even babies.

Yes, Jesus loves me!

"Wait!" said Jesus. "Let the little children come to me. Do not send them away. Children belong to God."

Yes, Jesus loves me!

The babies and sons and daughters got to see Jesus. Jesus touched them and blessed them. They knew that Jesus loved them.

Creative Fun

Make a copy of the heart for each child. Read the words on the heart and help each child write his or her name on the space provided. Have bits of lace, glitter, or torn tissue paper for the children to glue onto their hearts.

ZACCHAEUS

by Sharilyn Adair

the Bible

Luke 19:1-10

Jesus said, "Zacchaeus, hurry and come down; for I must stay at your house today."

(Luke 19:5, adapted)

Supplies

crayons
markers
tape
scissors
pen or pencil

Bible Story

The crowd was excited. "Here comes Jesus!" the people shouted. *(Point into the distance.)*

"Where?" Zacchaeus asked. He tried to see down the road, but people were all around him. Zacchaeus got bumped. *(Jerk your body to the left as though someone has bumped you.)* Zacchaeus got pushed. *(Jerk your body to the right as though someone has pushed you.)* And no one would talk to Zacchaeus.

Zacchaeus was sad. *(Frown.)* The people did not like Zacchaeus. He had taken their money and given it to the Romans. He had even kept some of the money for himself.

Even though Zacchaeus was bumped *(Jerk your body to the left as though someone has bumped you.)* and pushed *(Jerk your body to the right as though someone has pushed you.)*, he kept trying to see Jesus.

"I'll climb this tree!" *(Pretend to climb.)* Zacchaeus said. And up the tree he went.

Jesus came walking by. *(Walk in place.)* He smiled and waved at all the people. *(Smile and wave.)* Then Jesus looked up at Zacchaeus. *(Shade eyes with hand and look up.)* Jesus said, "Zacchaeus, hurry and come down *(Point to ground.)*, for I must stay at your house today."

Zacchaeus was happy! *(Smile.)* "Jesus, I want to be the people's friend. I will give back all the money I took for myself and even more." *(Pretend to hold a handful of coins.)*

"Good for you, Zacchaeus," Jesus said. "I have come to save people like you. Let's go to your house and eat." *(Walk in place.)*

creative Fun

Make a copy of the money bag and coins for each child. Fold the bag on the dotted line and tape it on both sides. Let the children decorate the bags. Cut out the coins for each child. Help the children think of kind things they can do for people. Help the children write those things on the coins. Let the children put the coins in their money bags.

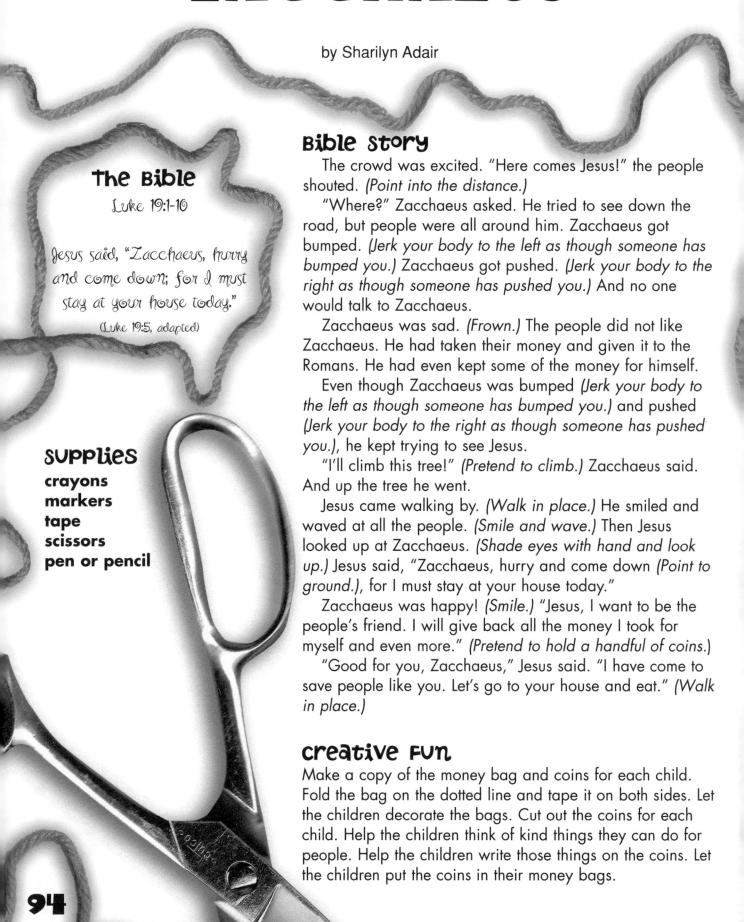

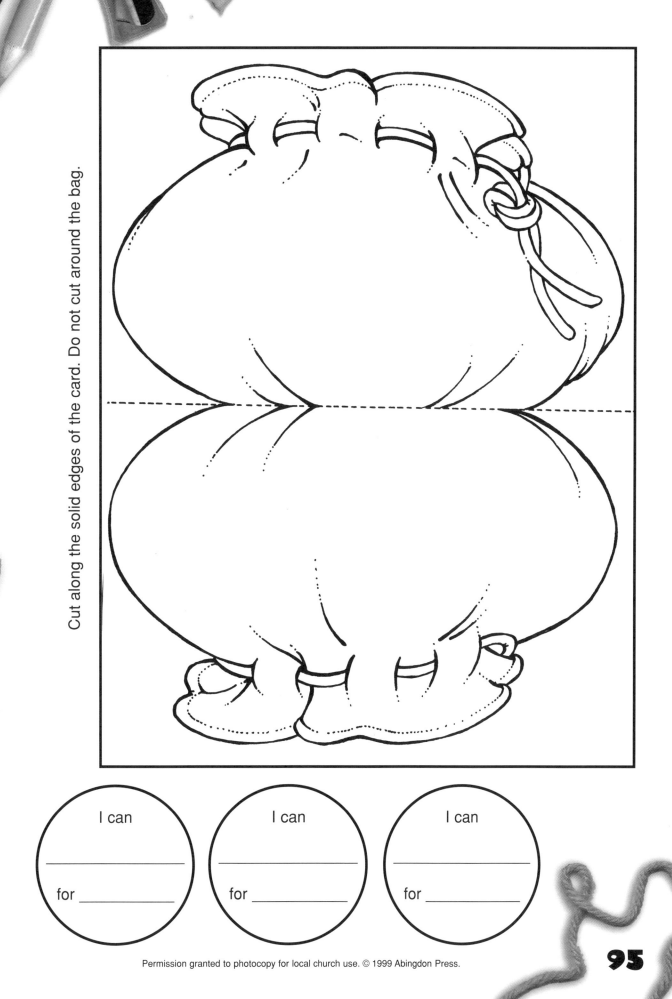

Cut along the solid edges of the card. Do not cut around the bag.

I can

_____

for _____

I can

_____

for _____

I can

_____

for _____

THE FOUR FRIENDS

by Daphna Flegal

The Bible

Luke 5:17-26; Mark 2:1-12

Love one another.

(John 15:17)

Supplies

scissors
crayons
markers
stapler or
tape
cotton balls

Bible Story

Once there was a man who could not walk. He had four friends who wanted to help him. "Jesus is in town," said the first friend. *(Hold up one finger.)* "He's telling people about God's love," said the second friend. *(Hold up two fingers.)* "Let's take our friend to see Jesus," said the third friend. *(Hold up three fingers.)* "We can carry him on a mat," said the fourth friend. *(Hold up four fingers.)*

The four friends laid the man on a mat. Each friend picked up a corner of the mat. They carried the man to the house where Jesus was talking to the people about God. But when they arrived, there were so many people that they could not get close to Jesus.

"Look at all the people," said the first friend. *(Hold up one finger.)* "There is no room for us to get into the house," said the second friend. *(Hold up two fingers.)* "We will never get close enough to Jesus," said the third friend. *(Hold up three fingers.)* "Wait, I have an idea," said the fourth friend. *(Hold up four fingers.)*

The four friends carried the man up the steps to the roof of the house. "Let's make a hole in the roof," said the first friend. *(Hold up one finger.)* "We can lower our friend through the hole," said the second friend. *(Hold up two fingers.)* "We can lay our friend on the floor," said the third friend. *(Hold up three fingers.)* "Right in front of Jesus," said the fourth friend. *(Hold up four fingers.)*

The four friends made a hole in the roof. Carefully they lowered their friend on the mat down, down to the floor right in front of Jesus. "Stand up!" Jesus said to the man on the mat. "Stand up and walk!"

The man stood up! He started to walk! He walked right out of the house!

"Praise God," said the first friend. *(Hold up one finger.)* "Praise God," said the second friend. *(Hold up two fingers.)* "Praise God," said the third friend. *(Hold up three fingers.)* "Praise God," said the fourth friend. *(Hold up four fingers.)*

CREATIVE FUN

Make two copies of this man for each child, one for the front and one for the back. Cut around the shapes. After the children color the man, staple or tape the two halves together, leaving an opening on one side. Let the children stuff the paper man with cotton balls. Then staple or tape the opening closed.

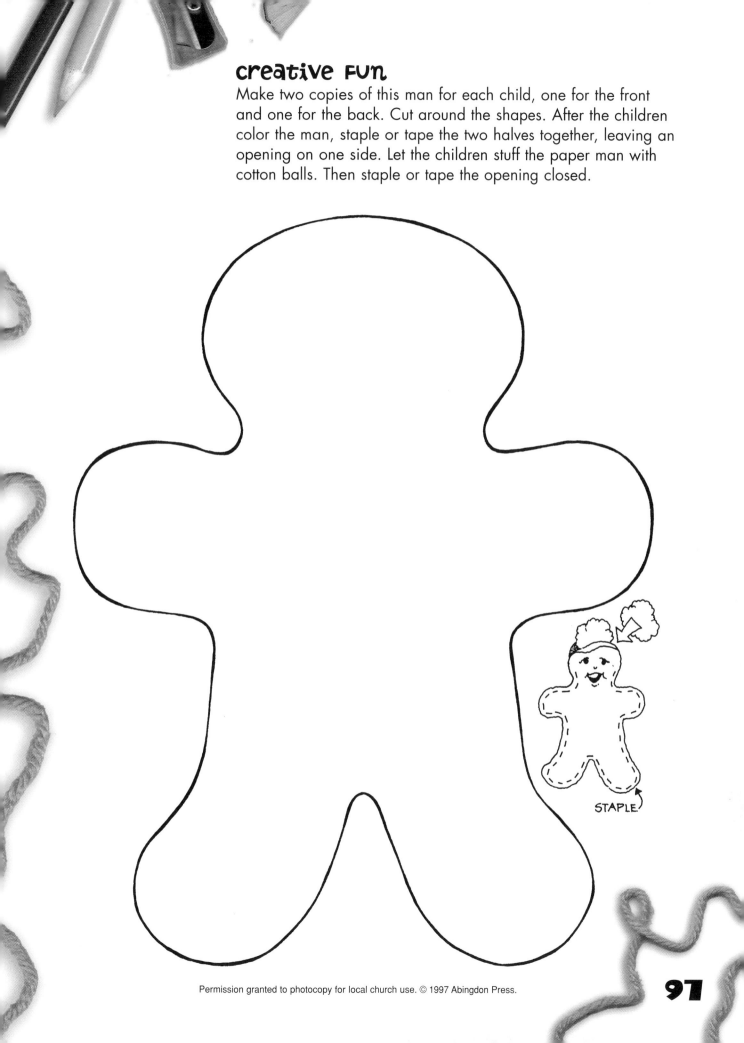

STAPLE

MARY AND MARTHA

by Judy Newman-St. John

the Bible

Luke 10:38-42

Teach me your way, O LORD.
(Psalm 86:11)

Supplies

crayons
markers
tape
paper
tissues
cotton balls

Bible story

Mary and Martha were sisters. They were friends of Jesus. One day Jesus came to Mary and Martha's house. Mary and Martha were very excited to see Jesus. He was their special guest.

Martha was very busy. She cleaned the house from top to bottom. She rolled up the sleeping mats. *(Pretend to roll up a mat.)* She swept the floor. *(Pretend to sweep.)* She carried fresh water from the well. *(Pretend to carry a heavy jar on your shoulder.)* She cooked a meal for Jesus. First she picked the fruit. *(Pretend to pick fruit.)* She baked the bread. *(Pretend to knead bread.)* She cooked some soup. *(Pretend to stir.)* She worked and worked.

Mary was not busy. She sat by Jesus. She listened to him teach about God's love.

Martha became upset! She wanted someone to help her with the work. *(Put hands on hips.)* "Jesus," Martha said. "I am so busy. Tell Mary to help me."

"Martha, Martha," answered Jesus. "All the work you are doing can wait. Come, sit down and listen. *(Pat beside you as if to have someone sit down.)* Mary is learning about God."

Martha wanted to learn more about God. She sat down beside Mary and listened to Jesus. Mary and Martha listened to Jesus' teachings and learned about God's love.

Creative Fun

Make two copies of the flower picture for each child to use to make a pillow. Have the children decorate the flowers. Help each child place the two papers together with the flowers facing out and tape them along three sides. Show the children how to stuff the pillow with crumpled paper, tissues, or cotton balls. Then tape the remaining side together. Have the children rest on their pillows while they hear stories of God's love.

99

HOSANNA!

by Sharilyn Adair

THE BIBLE

Mark 11:1-10

Hosanna!

(Mark 11:9)

SUPPLIES

scissors
markers
crayons
paper lunch
    bags
glue

CREATIVE FUN

Copy and cut out the parts of the donkey face for each child. Let the children color each part. Help the children glue the donkey's mouth underneath the bottom flap of a paper bag and the donkey's face on top of the bottom flap of the paper bag. Let the children glue the ears on either side of the face. Show the children how to place their hands inside the paper bag to make the donkey's mouth talk.

BIBLE STORY

Hee-haw! Hee-haw! I am Little Donkey. Let me tell you what happened to me! One day I was munching grass. My owner had me tied to a stake so I couldn't wander away and get lost. **Hee-haw! Hee-haw!**

Two men came up and untied me! **Hee-haw! Hee-haw!** I was afraid and called for my owner very loudly. **Hee-haw! Hee-haw!** He came right away.

"Why are you untying my donkey?" he asked them.

The men said, "The Lord needs your donkey. He will send it back to you when he is finished."

My owner decided that was okay, so I went with the men. When we got to a place outside the city, someone put a soft robe on my back. Then a man got up on my back and sat on the robe! **Hee-haw! Hee-haw!** I didn't know what to think of that! No one had ever ridden me before!

The man was kind and gentle with me. He talked to me in a soft voice. He guided me by my reins toward the city gates. Then things got pretty exciting!

People began to walk alongside us. They cheered, "Hosanna! Hosanna!" They threw their robes on the ground for me to walk over. They tore palm branches off the trees and waved them. "Hosanna! Hosanna!" they shouted.

I was so happy! Their shouts meant that the man who was riding me was some kind of king. I learned that his name was Jesus. I felt really special to be carrying him. Jesus rode me all the way to the Temple. "Hosanna!" Hosanna!" the people shouted. What an exciting day!

101

REMEMBER ME

by Elizabeth Parr

the Bible

Luke 22:7-20

Do this in memory of me.
(Luke 22:19,
Good News Translation)

supplies

crayons
markers
glue
purple and
brown
tissue
paper

Bible Story

Jesus and his friends were having a special meal together to celebrate Passover. Passover was a special time of celebration and remembering.

As Jesus and his friends ate together, Jesus held up a cup of grape juice. He thanked God for the juice. He asked his friends to drink from the cup and to remember him.

> **"Remember me, remember me."**
> **Were words that Jesus said.**
> **"Remember me, remember me."**
> **Come, share the juice and bread.**

Jesus also lifted up the bread. He thanked God for the bread. He asked his friends to eat the bread and to remember him.

> **"Remember me, remember me."**
> **Were words that Jesus said.**
> **"Remember me, remember me."**
> **Come, share the juice and bread.**

After they finished eating, Jesus and his friends sang a song together. The disciples knew that Jesus loved them. They would always remember Jesus and his love.

> **"Remember me, remember me."**
> **Were words that Jesus said.**
> **"Remember me, remember me."**
> **Come, share the juice and bread.**

Creative Fun

Make a copy of the Bible verse poster for each child. Let the children color the words of the verse. Have them glue small pieces of purple tissue paper on the cup and brown tissue paper on the bread.

Do this in memory of me.

Luke 22:19, Good News Translation

A ROOSTER CROWS

by Sharilyn Adair

The Bible

Luke 22:54-62

Jesus said,
"I call you friends."
(John 15:15,
Good News Translation, adapted)

Supplies

scissors

Bible Story

Peter was scared. Soldiers had arrested his friend Jesus. The soldiers had taken Jesus away to the high priest's house. Peter was afraid that the soldiers would arrest him too if they knew he was a friend of Jesus.

Crowds of people were outside the high priest's house. They were sitting around a bonfire and talking about Jesus and the soldiers. Oh, no! The people around the bonfire saw Peter. A woman pointed at Peter and said, "That man over there is with Jesus."

But Peter said, **"No! I do not know Jesus. He is not my friend!"** *(Have children cross arms over chest, stamp one foot, and shake head no.)*

Someone else said to Peter, "You are a follower of Jesus."

But Peter said, **"No! I do not know Jesus. He is not my friend!"** *(Have children cross arms over chest, stamp one foot, and shake head no.)*

Later another person said, "I know that man is a friend of Jesus. He is from the same country that Jesus is from."

But Peter said, **"No! I do not know Jesus. He is not my friend!"** *(Have children cross arms over chest, stamp one foot, and shake head no.)*

Just then Peter heard the rooster crow: **Cock-a-doodle-do!**

Oh, no! Peter felt terrible. He remembered that Jesus had told him, "Peter, you will say that you do not know me three times before the rooster crows." Peter had promised he would never do that, but now he had broken his promise. Peter knew that Jesus loved him. Jesus was his best friend.

Creative Fun

Make two copies of the rooster cards for each child, and cut them apart to make matching cards. Give each child a set. Have the children place their cards face down. Let them turn up two cards at a time to find cards that match. Have them place the matched cards to one side. As each child finds a pair of matched cards, have him or her crow: Cock-a-doodle-do!

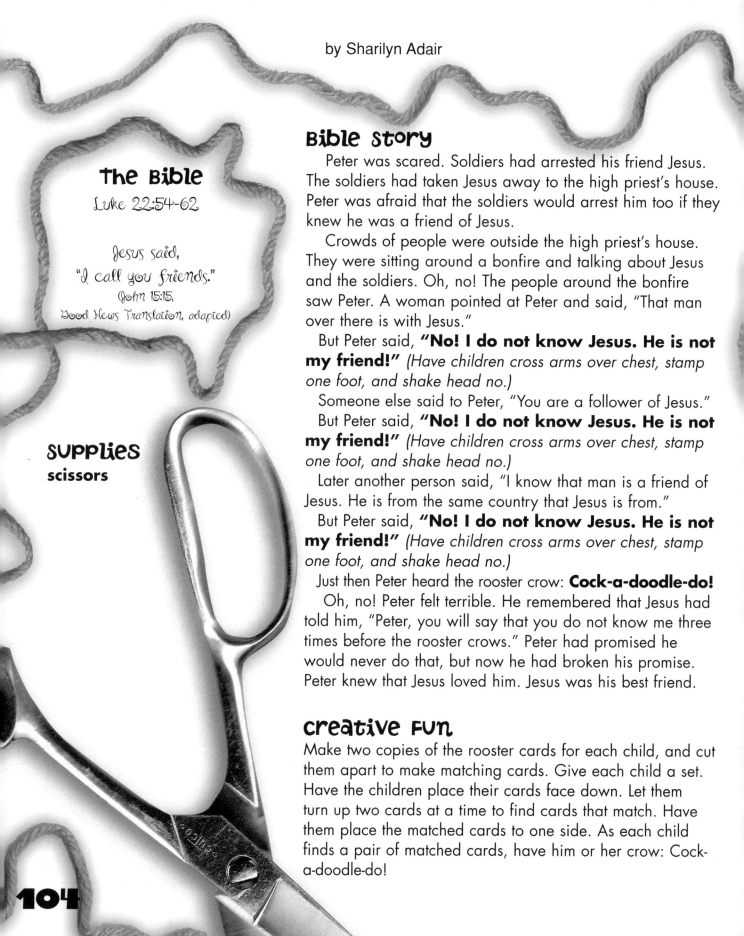

105

JESUS LIVES!

by Elizabeth Parr

the Bible

Luke 24:1-12

Sing happy songs in praise of the LORD.
(Psalm 98:4, CEV)

Supplies

plain white paper
white crayons
tempera paint
paintbrushes
water
shallow containers
coverups

Bible Story

It was Sunday morning and the sun was shining brightly. *(Pretend to shade eyes.)* The women were walking to the tomb. *(Walk in place.)* They were carrying the spices they had prepared for Jesus. *(Pretend to hold spices in hands.)*

When they came to the tomb, they were surprised. *(Open mouth and hold hands up in surprise.)* The stone had been rolled back from the entrance to the tomb! *(Pretend to roll stone.)*

The women crept inside the tomb. *(Creep.)* They looked around. *(Shade eyes and look around.)* Jesus was not there. *(Shrug shoulders and hold hands palms up.)*

Suddenly two angels stood beside the women. *(Make halo over head.)* The women were so frightened they fell to the ground. *(Kneel down to the ground.)* The angels told the women that Jesus was not there. *(Shake head no.)* Jesus is alive! *(Lift hands to sky.)*

The women remembered that Jesus had told them what would happen. *(Tap forehead.)* The women ran to tell Jesus' friends. *(Run in place.)* They were so happy! *(Smile and jump up and down.)* Jesus is alive! *(Lift hands to sky.)* Jesus is alive! *(Lift hands to sky.)*

Peter ran to the tomb to see if what they said was true. *(Run in place.)* Jesus was not there. *(Shake head no.)* Jesus is alive! *(Lift hands to sky.)* Jesus is alive! *(Lift hands to sky.)*

Creative Fun

Photocopy the butterfly to use as a tracing pattern. Cover the copy with a piece of plain white paper. Use a white crayon to trace the butterfly onto white paper for each child. Have the children use coverups. Use water to thin tempera paint in spring colors and pour the paint into shallow containers. Let the children brush the thinned paint all over their papers. The butterfly will show through the paint. Explain that the butterfly reminds us of the new life Jesus gives us.

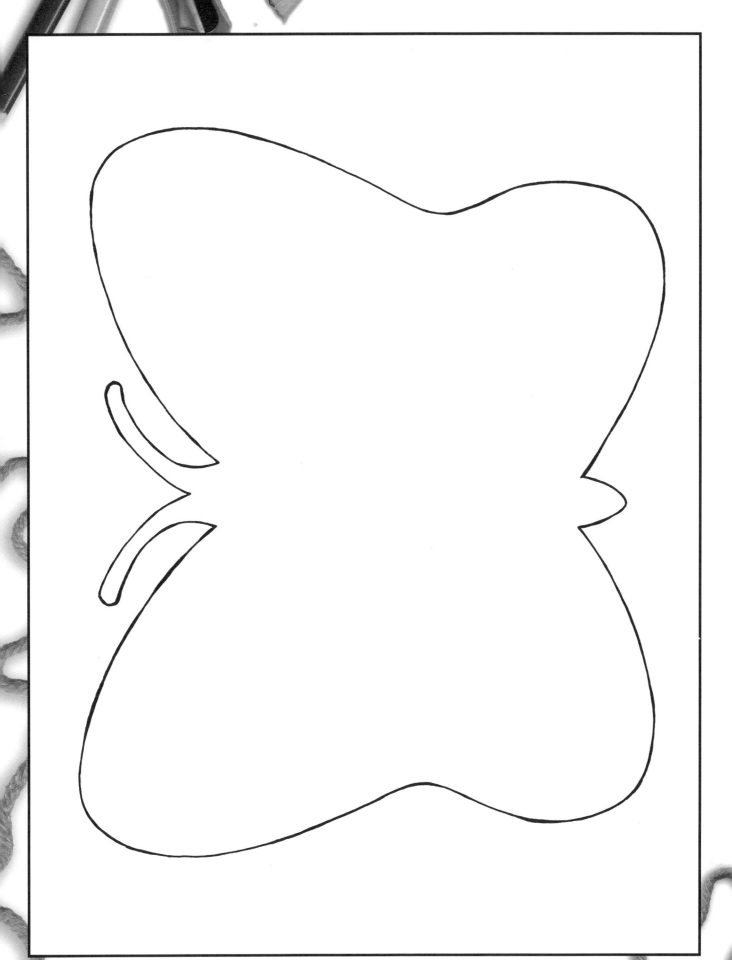

107

THE EMMAUS ROAD

by Judy Newman-St. John

the Bible

Luke 24:13-35

The Lord has risen indeed.
(Luke 24:34)

Supplies

scissors
crayons
markers
glue

Bible Story

Two men were walking down a road to a town called Emmaus. They were friends of Jesus. They were very sad. They thought their friend Jesus was dead.

As they were walking, they talked about Jesus. They were remembering the time they had spent with Jesus. They were remembering the special things Jesus had taught them. They were remembering everything that had happened in just the last few days.

A stranger started walking with them. They did not know who the stranger was. "What are you talking about as you are walking?" the stranger asked.

The two men looked at the stranger and wondered why he would ask such a question. "Don't you know what has happened? Have you not heard about our friend Jesus?" the men answered.

The stranger listened as the two men talked. "Our friend Jesus is dead," they said. "He was buried in a garden tomb. But early this morning some women went to the tomb. They saw that the stone had been rolled away and Jesus was not there."

As the three men walked along, the stranger listened to the two men. Then he started telling them about God, just like their friend Jesus used to do.

Soon the three men came to Emmaus. The two men invited the stranger to stay with them. They sat down to eat supper. The stranger took the bread from the table and broke it apart. He said a prayer to thank God for the bread. Then the two men knew who the stranger was! He was Jesus! Jesus was alive!

Creative Fun

Copy and cut out the card and happy message for each child. Have the children decorate the card and message with crayons and markers. Fold the card in half on the dotted line. Have the children glue the happy message inside the card.

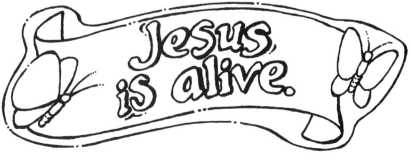

Jesus is alive.

ON THE BEACH

by Leedell Stickler

The Bible

John 21:1–14

Trust the Lord.
(Psalm 37:3, adapted)

Supplies

scissors
crayons
markers
yarn
tape

Bible Story

"It's a beautiful night," said Peter. "I think I'll go fishing."

"I'll go with you," said James.

"Good idea! We can help with the nets," said John.

The disciples pushed the boat out onto the lake. In the moonlight, they lowered their nets into the water. They held their torches high, hoping the fish would swim in.

"Time to haul in the nets," said Thomas. "We should have some fish by now." But when they pulled in the nets there wasn't a single fish. They decided to try again.

"One, two, three," and the men cast the net onto the surface of the lake. But when they pulled the net into the boat, it was empty. They tried over and over.

"We've been out here all night," said Peter. "We might as well go back."

The sun was just beginning to peek over the horizon. "Look," said Thomas, "there's someone on the beach. He's waving to us. What's he saying?"

"He says to cast the net on the right side of the boat. What have we got to lose?" So the men threw the net into the water on the other side of the boat. This time the nets were so full of fish that they almost turned the boat over.

"We'll have to drag the nets to shore," said James.

"Wait! That man on the shore! It's Jesus!" said Peter. Peter jumped into the water and swam to greet him.

Jesus had started a charcoal fire on the beach, ready to roast some of the fish the men had caught. "Come. Have breakfast," Jesus said to them. They could hardly believe their eyes.

Creative Fun

Make a copy of the hearts for each child to make a wall hanging. Cut around the hearts. Let the children decorate the hearts with crayons or markers. Help the children fold the heart in the middle. Place an 18-inch length of yarn inside the fold to create a hanger. Let the children tape the sides of the hearts together. Tie the ends of the yarn into a bow.

111

WIND AND FLAME

by Sharilyn Adair

The Bible

Acts 2:1-17

I will give my Spirit
to everyone.
(Acts 2:17, CEV)

Supplies

construction
paper
scissors
crayons
markers
glue

Bible Story

Whoosh! Whoosh! A special wind from God is blowing into the house where Jesus' followers are.

Whoosh! Whoosh! The wind blows all around the followers of Jesus. And they see something that looks like little flames of fire resting on them.

Whoosh! Whoosh! The followers feel the wind and see the flames. They remember their friend Jesus. They remember how sad they were when their friend Jesus died and how happy they were when they saw him alive again. They remember that Jesus had to go away but promised that something special would happen to help them feel God's love.

Whoosh! Whoosh! The wind helps them feel God's love. So The followers run out of the house to tell everyone they can find that Jesus is alive and wants everyone to ~~know that~~ remember God loves them.

Whoosh! Whoosh! Many people from ~~faraway places~~ all over the world are visiting Jerusalem. They are excited to see how excited the followers of Jesus are. They gather around to find out what is happening. The people listen, and everyone can understand what the followers are saying. They are glad to hear that Jesus is alive!

Whoosh! Whoosh! The people feel God's love. ~~Peter and the other followers baptize the people so they can be followers too.~~ Everyone is happy and wants to say thanks ~~you~~ for God's love.

↳ AMAZING

Creative Fun

Cut sheets of construction paper into three strips each. Copy and cut out a rainbow, church, and birthday cake for each child. Let the children color each piece. Give each child a strip of construction paper. Let the children glue the pieces onto the strip to create a Pentecost reminder. Explain to the children that Pentecost is when we celebrate the birthday of the church.

112

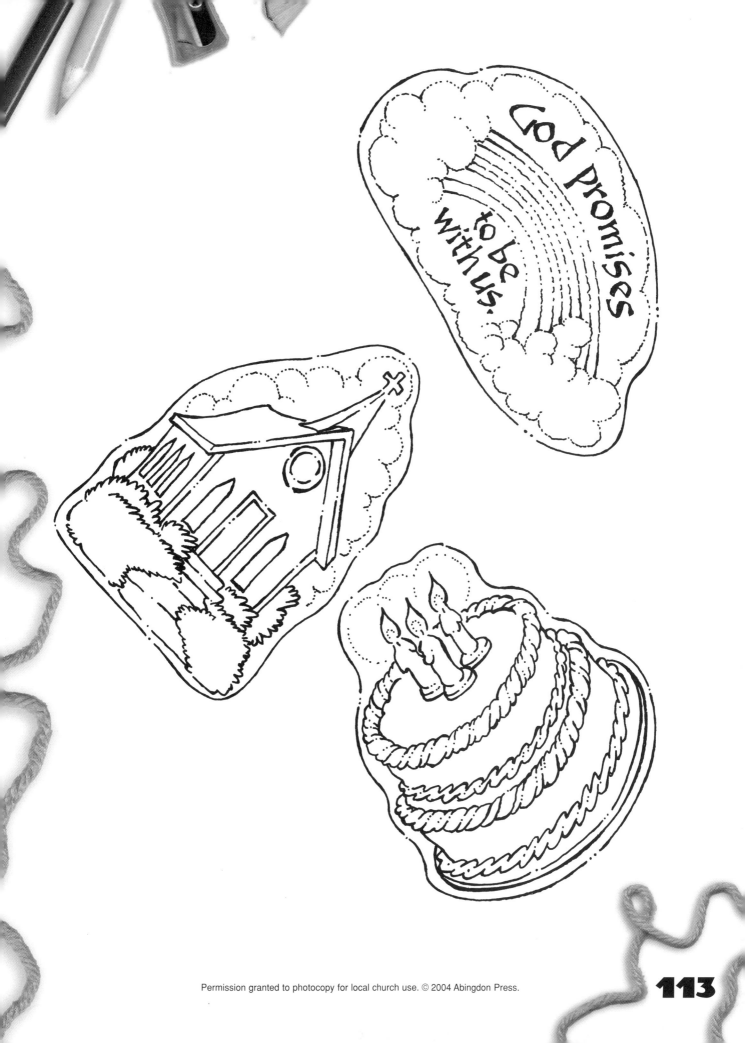

God Promises to be with us.

PETER AND JOHN

by Daphna Flegal

The Bible

Acts 3:1-10

Love is kind.

(1 Corinthians 13:4)

Supplies

scissors
markers
crayons
glue
yarn
tape
craft sticks
stapler and
staples

Bible Story

Peter and John were friends of Jesus. One day Peter and John were going to the Temple. As they walked by the gate of the Temple, they saw a man sitting on a mat.

"Please help me," said the man. "I cannot walk. I cannot work to have money for food. Please give me money so I can buy food to eat."

Peter and John stopped beside the man. They wanted to help him, but they had no money to give him.

"Look at us," said Peter.

The man looked up. He saw the two friends of Jesus.

"I don't have any silver or gold money," said Peter. "But I will give you something in the name of Jesus."

Peter took the man's hand. "Stand up and walk!" said Peter.

The man held on tight to Peter's hand. He stood up! The man felt his feet and ankles become strong.

"Praise God!" shouted the man. "I can walk!" The man walked into the Temple.

"Praise God!" shouted the man. "I can jump!" The man jumped around the Temple.

"Praise God!" shouted the man. "I can leap!" The man leaped around the Temple.

The people in the Temple saw the man leaping and jumping and praising God. "How did this happen?" they asked. "We knew this man could not walk."

Peter spoke to the people in the Temple. He said, "We helped this man walk in the name of Jesus."

Creative Fun

Copy and cut out the happy and sad faces for each child. Have the children decorate each face. Show them how to glue bits of yarn on for hair. Tape a craft stick to the back of one face. Help the children place the faces back to back and tape or staple around the edges to hold the faces together on the craft stick. Ask the children to use the faces to tell you how the man in the story felt.

115

Philip and the Ethiopian

by Sharilyn Adair

The Bible

Acts 8:26-38

Go, then, to all peoples everywhere and make them my disciples.
Matthew 28:19,
Good News Translation)

Supplies

scissors
crayons
markers
tape
yarn
glue

Bible Story

A man who was from a country far away was riding in a chariot. The man was reading from a scroll as he was riding in his chariot. The scroll that the man was reading had a book of the Bible written on it. The man knew about God, but he did not know about Jesus.

Go and tell, *(March in place.)*
Go and tell everyone about Jesus. *(Stop marching.)*

The friends of Jesus wanted everyone to know about Jesus. One of Jesus' friends was a man named Philip. Philip was standing by the road when the man in the chariot came riding by.

Go and tell, *(March in place.)*
Go and tell everyone about Jesus. *(Stop marching.)*

The man was reading out loud, and Philip could hear him. Philip ran up to the man's chariot. Philip asked, "Do you know what that book is about?"

"No," said the man. "I need someone to help me understand it." So the man invited Philip to ride with him in his chariot.

Philip told the man that the story he was reading was about how God had promised to send Jesus. Then Philip told the man all about Jesus. The man was glad to learn about Jesus. He was glad that he had asked Philip to ride with him in his chariot.

Go and tell, *(March in place.)*
Go and tell everyone about Jesus. *(Stop marching.)*

Creative Fun

Copy and cut out the horse and chariot cards for each child. Have the children draw a picture of the man in the chariot. Help the children tape the pictures together end to end so the horse is in front of the chariot. Create the reins by cutting a piece of yarn and gluing it to the horse's bridle and to the man's hands.

DAMASCUS ROAD

by Daphna Flegal

THE BIBLE

Acts 9:1-19

Love is kind.

(1 Corinthians 13:4)

SUPPLIES

scissors
tape

BIBLE STORY

"All the followers of Jesus should be put in jail," said Paul angrily. Paul was not a follower of Jesus. He did not know that **Love is kind.**

"I'm going to stop the followers of Jesus from telling others about Jesus," Paul said. "I'm going to another city to look for followers of Jesus." Paul was not a follower of Jesus. He did not know that **Love is kind.**

Paul started down the road. Suddenly Paul saw a very bright light. Paul was so surprised, he fell to the ground.

"Paul, Paul," said a voice from the light. "Why are you unkind to people who follow me?"

"Who are you?" asked Paul.

"I am Jesus," said the voice. "Go to the city. I will send someone to teach you what I want you to do."

Paul listened to Jesus. He was learning that **Love is kind.** Paul stood up. He could not see anything. Some of Paul's friends led him to the city. Paul stayed in the city three days.

A man named Ananias came to help Paul. "Paul, Jesus wants me to teach you how to be a follower of Jesus," said Ananias. He helped Paul to see again. Ananias helped Paul become a follower of Jesus. Paul learned that **Love is kind.**

Paul made a change. He became a follower of Jesus. He told many, many people the good news about Jesus. Paul wrote letters that told people about Jesus' love. Paul was a follower of Jesus. Paul knew that **Love is kind.**

CREATIVE FUN

Copy the change cards so that you have enough cards for at least two of the children to have the same card. Cut them apart. Tape a card to each child's clothing. Make sure the children understand what the cards represent. Have the children stand in a circle. Play a game as follows. Call out a card (for example, acorn) and the children wearing an acorn exchange places. Call out "everybody," and everybody exchanges places.

119

PAUL AND LYDIA

by Daphna Flegal

THE BIBLE

Acts 16:11-15

Love is kind.

(1 Corinthians 13:4)

SUPPLIES

crayons
markers
purple tissue
   paper
glue

Bible Story

Lydia sold purple cloth. Lydia liked the color purple. It was a special color. Only people who were rich could afford to buy purple cloth. Lydia was rich, and she was an important person in the city of Philippi.

Lydia loved God. She prayed to God every day. Lydia knew some other women who also loved God. They had no place to go in the city to pray to God, so Lydia and her friends met outside the city beside the river.

One day Lydia and her friends were sitting beside the river when a man named Paul came over to them.

Paul told Lydia and her friends all about Jesus. "Jesus is the Son of God," Paul said. "Jesus taught us that God loves us and will always be with us. Jesus taught us to be kind to one another and love one another. Jesus taught us that love is kind."

Lydia listened very carefully. Lydia was happy to learn about Jesus. Paul baptized Lydia in the river, and she became a follower of Jesus.

Lydia wanted her whole family to learn about Jesus. She invited Paul to stay at her house. Paul told Lydia's family about Jesus. Everyone at Lydia's house became a follower of Jesus.

Lydia still sold purple cloth. But now Lydia also helped others learn about Jesus.

Creative Fun

Make a copy of the picture of Lydia for each child. Have the children color the picture. Suggest they decorate Lydia's dress and cloth with purple crayons or glue on pieces of purple art tissue paper.

A LETTER FROM PAUL

by Sharilyn Adair

THE BIBLE

1 Corinthians 13

Love never ends.

(1 Corinthians 13:8)

SUPPLIES

scissors
markers
crayons
stapler and staples

Bible Story

A man named Paul wrote a letter to a church. His letter is in the Bible. His letter says:

Love is patient. *(Clap hands and say, "Yes! Yes! Yes!")* Is love taking someone else's turn? *(Stamp feet and say, "No! No! No!")* No, no! Love is patient. Love can wait. Love is happy for other people to have a turn.

Love is kind. *(Clap hands and say, "Yes! Yes! Yes!")* Is love pushing and shoving on the playground? *(Stamp feet and say, "No! No! No!")* No, no! Love is kind. Love does not hurt anyone else or make anyone else feel bad.

Love is not jealous; love does not want what others have. *(Clap hands and say, "Yes! Yes! Yes!")* Is love crying because I want Timothy's bear? *(Stamp feet and say, "No! No! No!")* No, no! Love is glad for others to have nice things. Love is thankful for my own things.

Love is not bragging; love does not think it is better than others. *(Clap hands and say, "Yes! Yes! Yes!")* Is love being glad that I am taller or can run faster than another child? *(Stamp feet and say, "No! No! No!")* No, no! Love wants everyone to be happy.

Love is not selfish. *(Clap hands and say, "Yes! Yes! Yes!")* Is love showing off my new toys and not letting others play with them? *(Stamp feet and say, "No! No! No!")* No, no! Love wants to share.

Love never ends. *(Clap hands and say, "Yes! Yes! Yes!")* Jesus will always love us. *(Clap hands and say, "Yes! Yes! Yes!")*

Creative Fun

Make a copy of the book for each child. Cut the pages apart on the solid lines. Have the children decorate each page. Help each child write his or her name in the space provided. Put the pages in order and staple them together on the left-hand edge. Read the book to the children.

Love never ends,

1 Corinthians 13:8

Love is kind,

1 Corinthians 13:4

Name

Paul's Little Instruction Book

123

SHIPWRECKED

by Sharilyn Adair

THE BIBLE

Acts 27

Love never gives up.
(1 Corinthians 13:7,
Good News Translation)

SUPPLIES

**crayons
markers
construction
paper
stapler and
staples
tissue paper or
newspaper**

Bible Story

Let's pretend we are on a big ship with Paul. Paul has been telling everyone about Jesus, and some people do not want to hear about Jesus. They made such a fuss that Roman soldiers had to come break up the fight. Paul and one of the soldiers are on their way to Rome so Paul can tell the emperor his side of the story.

First, let's walk up the gangplank onto the ship. *(Walk in place.)* My, we are getting up high. Let's put out our hands for balance. *(Put arms out to sides and weave torso back and forth as you continue to walk in place.)* Now we are at the side of the ship. Let's jump onto the ship. *(Jump once.)* We can stand at the side of the ship and look back to shore. *(Shade eyes with hands.)* The ship is beginning to move. Here we go! *(Start a gliding walk around the room.)*

At first we have a nice, smooth ride, but then the wind begins to blow, and the ship rocks up and down. *(Walk even more jerkily.)* The sailors throw the cargo overboard. *(Act as if throwing something over the side with both hands.)*

Paul has been praying. *(Fold hands in prayer.)* He says that the ship will have a wreck, but everyone will be all right. He says everyone should eat something for strength. *(Pretend to eat.)*

We see an island. *(Shade eyes with hands.)* Whoa! The ship is coming apart! We all fall in the water. *(Stoop to floor.)* Now we have to swim to shore. *(Stand up and make swimming motions with arms.)* Oh, we made it! Paul was right! God has been with us. We are all safe!

Creative Fun

Make a copy of the Bible verse page for each child. Have the children decorate the page with crayons and markers. Give each child a piece of construction paper. Place the Bible verse page on top of the construction paper and staple three edges of the pages together, leaving a fourth edge open. Let the children stuff tissue paper or crumpled newspaper in the opening. Staple the fourth edge together to complete the pillow.

Love never gives up.
1 Corinthians 13:7
Good News Translation

SCRIPTURE INDEX

Old Testament

SCRIPTURE INDEX

New Testament

Development Editor: Judith A. Newman-St. John
Production Editor: David Whitworth
Production and Design Manager: R.E. Osborne
Designer: Paige Easter
Illustrator: Robert S. Jones
Writers: Sharilyn Adair, Peg Augustine, Anita Edlund,
    Daphna Flegal, Judy Newman-St. John,
    Elizabeth Parr, and Leedell Stickler

Sharilyn Adair: Pages 28, 30, 74, 94, 100, 104 © 1998 Abingdon Press.
Pages 6, 8, 10, 52, 116, 122, 124 © 1999 Abingdon Press. Pages 16,
18, 44, 112 © 2000 Abingdon Press.

Peg Augustine: Pages 60, 68, 70 © 1997 Abingdon Press.

Anita Edlund: Page 78 © 2005 Abingdon Press.

Daphna Flegal: Pages 12, 48, 50, 54, 80, 92, 96, 114, 118, 120 © 1997
Abingdon Press. Pages 22, 40, 82, 84, 86 © 1998 Abingdon Press.
Pages 56, 72 © 1999 Abingdon Press.

Judy Newman-St. John: Pages 62, 66, 76, 88, 98, 108 © 2005
Abingdon Press.

Elizabeth Parr: Pages 24, 36, 64, 90, 102, 106 © 2003 Abingdon
Press. Pages 14, 20, 26, 32, 34, 38, 42 © 2004 Abingdon Press.

Leedell Stickler: Pages 46, 58, 110 © 2005 Abingdon Press.